Alan

DIEPKLOOF

Reflections of Diepkloof Reformatory

WRITINGS COMPILED & EDITED BY
CLYDE BROSTER

Happy Birthday to a Soul Brother!
Love from
Mum.   30-7-92.

DAVID PHILIP
Cape Town   Johannesburg

Grateful acknowledgments are due to Jonathan Cape Ltd, London, for permission to include extracts from *Debbie Go Home* (1961) and *Kontakion for You Departed* (1969).

The other three books from which extracts have been taken, *Knocking on the Door: Shorter Writings* (1975) by Alan Paton, *Towards the Mountain: An Autobiography* (1980) by Alan Paton, and *Sponono: A Play in Three Acts* (Africasouth Paperbacks 1983) by Alan Paton and Krishna Shah, were published by David Philip, Publisher (Pty) Ltd, Cape Town.

FOURTH IMPRESSION 1990

This collection first published 1986 in Southern Africa by David Philip, Publisher (Pty) Ltd, Werdmuller Centre, Claremont, Cape, 7700 South Africa

ISBN 0 86486 043 9

© Alan Paton 1986
© selection Clyde Broster 1986

Printed and bound by Creda Press (Pty) Ltd, Solan Road, Cape Town, South Africa

Contents

Foreword	v
To a Small Boy Who Died at Diepkloof Reformatory	1
(from *Knocking on the Door*)	
The Gift	3
(from *Knocking on the Door*)	
First Days at Diepkloof	7
(from *Towards the Mountain* and *Kontakion for You Departed*)	
Experiment in Freedom	16
(from *Kontakion for You Departed* and *Towards the Mountain*)	
Final Transformations	22
(from *Towards the Mountain* and *Kontakion for You Departed*)	
Ha'penny	33
(from *Debbie Go Home*)	
The Divided House	38
(from *Debbie Go Home*)	
Death of a Tsotsi	44
(from *Debbie Go Home*)	
The Worst Thing of His Life	51
(from *Debbie Go Home*)	
Sponono	56
(from *Debbie Go Home*)	
The Court	70
(from *Sponono: A Play*)	
Appendix: Some Thoughts on Education and Reform	96
(from *Knocking on the Door* and *Towards the Mountain*)	

Foreword

Dr Alan Paton is internationally known as an author and politician, but it is as an educationist that this collection attempts to portray him, since this has been his sphere of most direct influence upon me personally. Before the publication of *Cry, the Beloved Country* brought him worldwide fame in 1948, Dr Paton had been a teacher of mathematics and science at Ixopo High School and Maritzburg College, and Principal of Diepkloof Reformatory. His reminiscences, published from time to time, are so full of insight, compassion, and practical wisdom, that I asked for permission to edit and gather together into one volume those of his writings which had a specifically educational bearing, and which were valuable to me for their narrative skill and inspirational philosophy. This permission was promptly and graciously given.

For the documentary sections of the book, I have primarily followed *Kontakion for You Departed*, Dr Paton's beautiful tribute addressed to his first wife, Dorrie, and published two years after her death; but I have interpolated explanatory paragraphs from the formal autobiography *Towards the Mountain*. Short stories have been included from *Knocking on the Door* and *Debbie Go Home*. The main body of the book closes with an abbreviated excerpt from the courtroom sequence of a play by Alan Paton and Krishna Shah, in which the Principal is called upon to account for his actions. I trust that, in selecting and arranging these passages, I have been able to do so in order to make them fit together coherently in their new context, and that no great damage has been done to Dr Paton's original intentions; and I trust, too, that my admiration for them will be shared by any whose lives have been affected by the teaching-and-learning process.

Clyde Broster
Rondebosch

To a Small Boy Who Died at Diepkloof Reformatory

Small offender, small innocent child
With no conception or comprehension
Of the vast machinery set in motion
By your trivial transgression,
Of the great forces of authority,
Of judges, magistrates, and lawyers,
Psychologists, psychiatrists, and doctors,
Principals, police, and sociologists,
Kept moving and alive by your delinquency,
This day, and under the shining sun
Do I commit your body to the earth
Oh child, oh lost and lonely one.

Clerks are moved to action by your dying;
Your documents, all neatly put together,
Are transferred from the living to the dead,
Here is the document of birth
Saying that you were born and where and when,
But giving no hint of joy or sorrow,
Or if the sun shone, or if the rain was falling,
Or what bird flew singing over the roof
Where your mother travailed. And here your name
Meaning in white man's tongue, he is arrived,
But to what end or purpose is not said.

Here is the last certificate of Death;
Forestalling authority he sets you free,
You that did once arrive have now departed
And are enfolded in the sole embrace
Of kindness that earth ever gave to you.

So, negligent in life, in death belatedly
She pours her generous abundance on you
And rains her bounty on the quivering wood
And swaddles you about, where neither hail nor tempest,
Neither wind nor snow nor any heat of sun
Shall now offend you, and the thin cold spears
Of the highveld rain that once so pierced you
In falling on your grave shall press you closer
To the deep repentant heart.

Here is the warrant of committal,
For this offence, oh small and lonely one,
For this offence in whose commission
Millions of men are in complicity
You are committed. So do I commit you,
Your frail body to the waiting ground,
Your dust to the dust of the veld, –
Fly home-bound soul to the great Judge-President
Who unencumbered by the pressing need
To give society protection, may pass on you
The sentence of the indeterminate compassion.

The Gift

I had not long been at school. I was six years old and clever, and it was not long before I distinguished myself indoors. But outdoors in the playground I was quiet and gentle, and stood against the brick walls in the sun, watching them play. I would have played had they asked me to, but no one did, so I kept myself to myself.

I remember one occasion on which I attracted attention. I wore a pair of shoes that did not lace up, but had a strap that went over the instep and was fastened by a button. These shoes some knowing fellows pronounced to be girls' shoes, but I denied it, not hotly or angrily, but no doubt quietly and gently. I had no idea that such a small matter could attract such great attention, but soon there was a crowd of boys around me, and the knowing ones again pronounced the shoes to be girls' shoes. They were supported, too, by all the other knowing and manly and strong-looking boys, and indeed by all those who spoke at all, for no one spoke a word on my behalf. So I spoke for myself, quietly and gently, that these were boys' shoes. Then a big and manly and strong-looking boy angrily put his arm length-wise in front of his chest, and if he had flung it out he would have caught me in the face. I could not shrink against the wall because I had my back to it already, and whether some pity was excited in him or whether he was afraid of authority I do not know, but he brought his arm down again and contented himself by asserting again that these were girls' shoes and by looking at me to see if I would deny it. But I did not deny it again.

Maybe I was too meek to satisfy whatever desire they might have had, for they drifted away and left me, and left some others, too, not so manly or strong-looking as those who had gone, but not so quiet and gentle as myself. One of them said, when the others were safely gone, 'Those are not girls' shoes,' and I smiled at him timidly and gratefully. Perhaps he saw that I might have attached myself to him, and perhaps he had no wish and even some fear to go any further, for he, too, left me, and there I was standing alone, thinking only to myself, these shoes look like girls' shoes. I lifted one foot and put it on the other, so hiding one shoe, but the other could not be hidden, and I thought of some plan to hide them both.

I walked along to the big school verandah and sat down there on one of the benches, for there I could put both my feet under the bench, and thus hide the shoes. But I had not been sitting there long when a teacher came to me and said, 'Sitting, sitting, go and play in the sun.' She said, 'Aren't you well?' but I had no great experience of telling lies, so I told her I was well, and she said, 'Then go into the sun, it's against the rules to sit here now.'

That is what I was like. But this is not really my story. My story is stranger than that. It has stayed with me all my life, and keeps on coming back to me, two or three times every year, at times perhaps when I think too much about myself. It has not always done that; for many years it lay sleeping in the depths of my memory, and then suddenly I remembered it. When I first remembered it, it astonished me, and filled me with pain and shame and pity. I write it down now because it seems foolish to feel pain and shame about it. The pity I feel still, but the astonishment is gone, not quite gone, but turned into a kind of wonder at what went on in the mind of a quiet child put out into the world.

It was another day at school. I stood in my usual place against the wall and the playground was full of the cries and calls of boys playing and pushing. They, and I in much smaller measure, had got used to the shoes that looked like girls' shoes, and they left me in peace.

Near where I stood, a gate opened out into the street, and I could see all the people that passed by the school. It was the middle of the day, and we had all eaten the food, usually sandwiches, that our mothers gave us to bring. But it was poor food for a day like this, for without warning a wind had sprung up and the weather had suddenly turned cold and bitter. Yet it was with dismay that I saw coming up the street towards the gate of the school, the black boy who worked as a servant in our house. He carried a basket, and over the top of the basket was a clean white cloth. I knew at once that it was food, no doubt hot food, that my mother had sent because of the sudden bitterness of the day. And I knew, too, that this would attract more attention to me and embarrass me, so I went further along the wall so as not to be seen by the boy. I had not been standing there long when one of the schoolboys came to me and said, 'Your boy's here, with a basket.'

'What boy?' I asked.

'Your boy,' he said. 'The boy that works at your house.'

I shook my head, denying finally and completely that such a boy could be there.

'I'll bring him to you,' he said.

So he brought the boy, and of course it was our boy, and we both knew it as well as any two human beings could, but while he smiled at me uncertainly because of the strangeness of the place, I shook my head.

'That's not our boy,' I said.

Some of the schoolboys spoke to him, and I heard him telling them privately, not openly, because my attitude confused him, that he was certainly my mother's boy, and that I was certainly the young master of the house, and that my mother had sent me something warm to eat and drink. But I denied it resolutely.

Then one of the schoolboys brought him nearer with his basket and took off the white cloth, and there was a jug with a cup in the mouth of it, and another white cloth in which something was wrapped up. The schoolboy took the cup out of the mouth of the jug, and it was steaming.

'Cocoa!' he said, smelling it. 'Hot cocoa!'

He opened the second white cloth, and there were the scones that my mother had baked. And I knew that while they were hot she had opened them, not with a knife but with her fingers, and had dropped butter into them, to melt and sink yellow and sweet, into their very hearts. Even then, as I now remember, I thought of my mother thinking of me at school, and I was touched and therefore ashamed, but I resolutely denied that this was our boy, and so denied that it was my mother's work. And by this time all the attention that I feared had been directed at me, and at the black servant and the cocoa and the scones, so that half the school was there, watching the strange spectacle of a boy who would not claim so timely and desirable a gift.

Then one of the manly and strong-looking boys said to me, 'Come on, it's your mother's boy.'

But I denied it.
Then he said, 'What are you going to do with it?'
'It's not mine,' I said.
'Can I have it?' he asked.
'It's not mine,' I said stubbornly.
'Can I have it?' he asked again.

So persistent was he in asking my permission that he forced me to acknowledge some kind of ownership, and at last I said unwillingly, 'It's not mine, but you can have it.'

So he shared it with his friends, the cocoa and the scones. Our black boy held the basket patiently, and what he thought of it I do not know. When they had finished he put the jug and the cup back into the basket and covered them with the white cloth. Then he saluted me and went out of the gate down the street. But, of course, I did not acknowledge his salute, for what had I to do with this unknown boy?

Then the schoolbell rang, and I went back indoors with relief, where whatever attention I attracted would be warm and pleasurable.

As I remember, my mother asked me when I returned if this strange story was true, and I did not lie to her, as I had done to the boys at school. I do not remember that she spoke any further; I do not remember that she patted my head or smiled in any special way at me; I do not remember that she ever told the story to my father or my brother, but I am almost sure she did not, because my brother would have plagued me with it. I have no doubt that she kept it in her heart.

And so would any mother keep it in her heart. For this is one for whom she fears, going forward and retreating, now confident, now afraid, making his way from her womb into the world.

First Days at Diepkloof

In 1934 I spent seventy-seven days in hospital with typhoid. In those days the treatment for typhoid was starvation, and I wasted away, losing fifty of my hundred and fifty pounds. Twice you came to take me home, because I was thought to have recovered, and each time they took my temperature, and sent me back to bed at once. The second time I broke down and wept; I thought I would never go home again. You hid your own disappointment, and tried to comfort me. Your preparations for my homecoming, in which kind of task you excelled, the special food, the books, the visits from family and friends, the hundred things you had arranged to give me pleasure, all came to nothing.

When at last I came out, I had great difficulty in walking. I sat in the garden in the autumn sun, and you waited on me, as they say, hand and foot. When I could walk, I went one day to town, and in Church Street the father of one of the boys I taught at Maritzburg College stopped me and asked, 'What are you going to do now?' I said, 'I'm going back to school.' He said, 'You won't stay there long; after an illness like that, you'll do something new.' And he was right. A few months after that I applied for the principalship of one of the three reformatories, Tokai, Houtpoort, and Diepkloof.

In 1934 Parliament decided to transfer all reformatories from the Department of Prisons to the Union Department of Education, with the intention of replacing a penal objective by a reformatory one. The fact that the word 'reformatory' was used at all was an acknowledgement that the institution had an educational as well as a custodial function. In the reformatories for white boys there was a programme of instruction in the 'trades', such as building, carpentry and cabinet-making, metalwork, and painting; in the reformatory for coloured boys, there was also some trade instruction, but a great many of them worked on the lands of the historical estate of Tokai, on the periphery of Cape Town. In the reformatory for African boys, all of them worked on the lands of the beautiful farm known as Diepkloof, just outside Johannesburg. There was a theory – not unknown in other countries – that the land exercised some mystical therapeutic influence on juvenile offenders. This theory could be carried to absurd lengths, and continued to be held even when more than ninety percent of juvenile offenders placed on the land ran away from it to get back to the lights and the sounds of the cities.

The Union Department of Education naturally decided to appoint as principals of its new institutions men and women from the world of education. Four posts for men were advertised, two for the white reformatories at Tokai and Houtpoort, one for the coloured reformatory at Tokai, and one for the African reformatory at Diepkloof, on the outskirts of Johannesburg. I wrote a private letter to Mr J. H. Hofmeyr, Minister of Education, and told him that I would like to get a post at a reformatory.

Why did I decide to take such a step? One reason was undoubtedly the restlessness caused in me by my long illness and my long absence from school. Another was undoubtedly ambition. But a third reason was that I was attracted by the idea of working with young offenders.

I did not have to wait long for an answer to my letter to Mr Hofmeyr. His fame for swift replies was immense. His custom was to keep all unanswered letters in the inside pocket of his jacket, and therefore swift reply was essential. This habit was extremely bad for the smartness of the jacket, but that did not worry him.

In his reply he advised me to apply for all the four principalships, Tokai White and Tokai Coloured, Houtpoort White and Diepkloof African. He told me I would not get Tokai White because it was intended for a man who was already a principal in the Union Education Department. As for Diepkloof African, he had been to see it himself, and he wrote, 'It is hard to know what can be done with it.' I therefore applied for all four principalships, hoping that I would not get Diepkloof.

But that is what I got. I took the letter into the garden, and tried to summon up courage to tell you. When at last I told you, you were much distressed, and would not be comforted. You said to me tearfully, 'What do you know about reformatories? What do you know about African delinquents? Why do we have to leave Natal, where all our family and friends are? I don't want to go.'

That was one of the occasions when I could not go up to you and comfort you, because we were estranged by this event. It was the only time in your life that you did not want to accompany me. You did not want to leave the security of Pietermaritzburg, and that countryside of mist and grass and bracken, you did not want to venture into the unknown world of the Transvaal and reformatories and delinquency and who knew what else. But I was excited about it. At the age of thirty-two I was being given the chance of turning a prison into a school, I was being given a school of my own. Up till my illness I had hoped one day to be made the headmaster of Maritzburg College, probably at the age of fifty. Instead I went off to Diepkloof at thirty-two, not soberly as I no doubt should have done, but a trifle light-heartedly. I am sure that none of this helped you to overcome your feeling of hurt, because I had, without visible signs of regret, overturned your world. It was more than a month before you followed me.

July 1935. My first month at Diepkloof Reformatory, as foul a place as ever I saw. Four hundred boys were housed in wood-and-iron buildings set round a hollow square, one side of which was used for administration. Round the entire block, and about twenty feet from it, ran a thirteen-foot-high barbed-wire fence, inclining at an angle towards the building.

In this block was a great gate, and opposite it was a corresponding gate in the high fence, and the two gates might not be open simultaneously, except when the whole reformatory marched out to work at 8.00 a.m. and 1.00 p.m. or when it marched back again at noon and 4.00 p.m. At the gates were men in uniform, and when I arrived they greeted me with quivering salutes, impassive faces, and a thundering of heavy boots on the concrete as they came to attention. The outside of the huge block was closed and blind, except for high windows heavily barred. Four hundred boys lived in the block in about twenty rooms, the doors of which opened on to the hollow square. Just after five o'clock in the afternoon, when they had had their supper, they assembled together for evening prayers, and sang as beautifully as any four hundred boys ever sang upon the earth. Then they paraded outside their rooms and were counted. Then they paraded inside their rooms and were counted again. Then they were locked in for fourteen hours, with one bucket full of water and another bucket for urination and defecation. The lights burned all night, and in each door was a spy hole through which acts of turpitude could be observed. The stench which poured out of the rooms when the doors were opened at 7.00 a.m. was unspeakable.

DIEPKLOOF REFORMATORY MAIN BLOCK

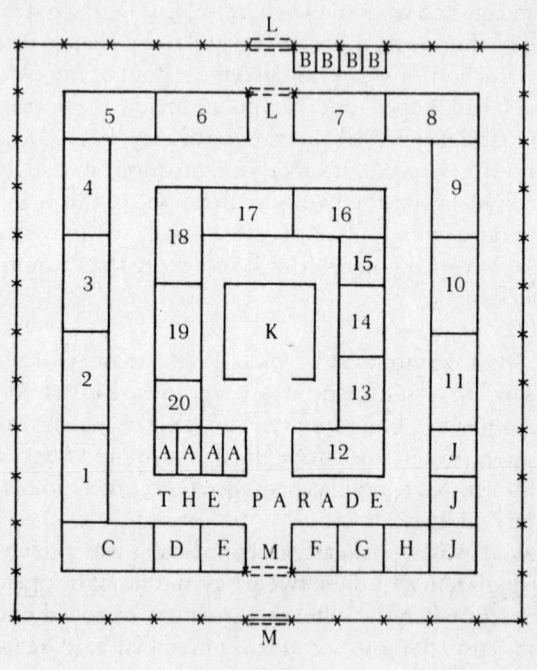

LEGEND

1–20 – Dormitories
x – Iron stanchions supporting security fence
A – Solitary Confinement cells
B – Hospital Isolation cells
C – Yard stores
D – Warden
E – Deputy Warden

F – Main office
G – Storeman
H – Bulk stores
J – Hospital
K – Kitchen
L–L – Gates for exit of dirt, sewage, etc.
M – Main gates

The opening of the cells preceded the first count of the day. This business of the count was probably the most important in the entire routine of managing a custodial institution. Some twenty shivering boys paraded in front of each foul room, clad in nothing but shirt and short trousers. An iron discipline was exercised, but not the greatest disciplinarian could have stopped the boys from shivering. They were silent but the staff were not, especially the black warders in their black serge uniforms, and armed with heavy sticks. Commands and rebukes and what came close to curses filled the air, and the sound of blows could be heard, though I do not remember to have seen one on this my first working day.

After this parade the boys adjourned to the watertaps situated throughout the yard. The water was cold, and in July it was ice-cold. But there was no pretence of cleanliness during the weeks. On Saturday afternoon hot water was distributed in metal basins, but there was no question of a bath.

Then came breakfast, which consisted of mealie-meal porridge and black coffee. The boys collected dish and mug and spoon and filed into the kitchen for their rations. These they took back to that portion of the yard which on the plan is called the parade, and after grace they ate sitting on the ground.

After breakfast they paraded, each in his appointed place. The group with which each boy paraded was called his *span*, which is the Afrikaans word for 'team' or 'gang'. Afrikaans was the language of the reformatory; most of the white personnel was Afrikaans-speaking, but above and beyond that, Afrikaans is, except in southern Natal, the language of the African delinquent. It is a weird and wonderful Afrikaans, far from pure and certainly far from holy, but full of the vitality of the slums of the cities.

When all the boys had paraded with their *spans*, they were counted. If the count proved correct, the two gates were opened and the *spans* marched out to work on the reformatory farm, the numbers again being counted by the officer on duty at the gate. At noon they returned, and were counted in. After their midday meal they had half an hour of rest, and again, on the ringing of the bell, paraded with their *spans* and were counted, marched out with their *spans* and were counted, returned at 4.00 p.m. with their *spans* and were counted. At 4.30 p.m. they had their evening meal of mealie-meal porridge, a stout piece of bread, and black coffee. At 5.00 p.m.

evensong was held, taken by Head Teacher Moloi. The boys sang a hymn, and the beauty of it, and the earnestness and innocence and reverence of those four hundred delinquent voices, captured me then and held me captive for thirteen years. I may add that it captured many others also, and sometimes visitors to the reformatory could hardly hold back their tears. Then Moloi read a short passage of scripture, and prayed briefly, after which the whole reformatory recited 'Our Father' in Zulu. Moloi pronounced the benediction and the warden or his deputy said, 'Goodnight, boys,' and the congregation said, 'Goodnight, sir.' The boys then assembled in front of their rooms, and were counted for the last time of the day. Then they were locked in with their two buckets, and the reformatory was handed over to two night warders.

These countings, these locked doors, these double gates, and the high fence that ran round the whole block, had naturally one purpose and one only, and that was to prevent the inmates from running away. How was this one purpose to be reconciled with, or at least to operate alongside of, an educational and reformatory purpose? That was the problem that I had to solve somehow, for if I did not solve it, then I would have proved myself a fool for ever having undertaken to do so. And there was another problem, practical and urgent. What was I to do about those buckets in the rooms? It was unthinkable that I should allow such a thing to continue.

Meanwhile I was saluted and stamped at continuously. I was treated as though I were an emperor of some immense domain. Yet this was all a facade. Behind it sixty pairs of eyes were watching me, sixty men, some of them prison officers with many years of service, watching this young schoolmaster of thirty-two, who perhaps had never before seen a delinquent in his life, who could not have clapped a pair of handcuffs on anybody if he had tried, who had no doubt read many books in the silence of a sequestered study. How would he make of this grim foul padlocked encircled and potentially dangerous place, anything that might be called a school?

I now knew what Mr Hofmeyr meant when he had written, 'It is hard to know what can be done with it.' I had only three cards of any value; one was an overwhelming determination to do something with it, the second was an aptitude for wrestling with problems, and the third was a physical energy that amazes me when I look back on it.

There is a last element, but I don't think I can call it an asset. It was luck. I was to have many disappointments and suffer many anxieties, but I was never struck the kind of blow from which I would never be able to recover, the kind of blow that exposes the vain ambitious young man with the high purpose as nothing more than a self-deluded fool, playing with forces the strength and nature of which he just did not understand.

My first days at Diepkloof were days of exhilaration. Freedom was hardly the characteristic of this grim reformatory, but I had an extraordinary sense of it. For one thing I was no longer tied to a teaching timetable. Yet I would be down at the yard at 7.30 a.m. for the breakfast parade and for the work parade at 8.00 a.m. After the boys' work had begun I would go home for breakfast, and after that would go walking on the farm, visiting the various teams of boys and their supervisors. Our son David was now five years old, and his companions were the small boys of the reformatory. He was given a *span* of his own, and marched it in and out of the gate. Our second son, Jonathan, actually grew up at the reformatory, and the playmates of his later childhood were also the small boys. In fact the reformatory was our home and our life.

The respect shown to me was excessive. This had nothing to do with my character or personality, but was paid to my office. It was in fact the tradition of prisons. When I visited a *span*, supervisor and boys would come to attention with military precision. The parade was in fact an important instrument of order and discipline, and indeed it would have been impossible to organise such a large number of boys without it. There were the breakfast and other meal parades, the work parades at 8.00 a.m. and 1.00 p.m. and the evensong parade at 5.00 p.m. The parades were in fact the events of the day, and their role was made all the more important because we had no assembly hall and no dining hall.

After this walk in the freedom of the highveld air, at a time when all my colleagues at Maritzburg College would be incarcerated in their classrooms, I would return to the main building and attend to the mail of the day, which was always tremendous, and dealt with committals, releases, relapses, probation reports, and all staff matters.

With few exceptions the staff members had all been members of the Prison Service, and many of them were waiting to return to it. It was only a few days after my arrival that three new white staff members arrived to take the place of three warders who had elected to stay with the Prisons Department. These three were young men in their very early twenties, and had been members of a unit called the Special Service Battalion. Although they were in civilian clothes, they came into my office and came to attention with a deafening crash that threatened to bring down the building. So these young Afrikaners came to a job of a kind they had never dreamt of, that of being supervisors at a black reformatory, and of helping in the re-education and rehabilitation of black delinquent boys. But if it had not been for these young sergeants and sergeants-major, and all the others from the battalion who followed them, Diepkloof Reformatory would never have been changed from a prison into a school.

The arrival of the battalion young men enabled me to do one thing, that was to forbid all shouting in the yard by members of the staff. Gone were the shouting, the anger, the rebuking, that had been the outward signs of the hidden conflict between age and youth, between officer and boy, which is the mark of every bad school, penal or otherwise. The young men from the battalion did not find it necessary. They transformed the parades from subdued affairs interrupted only by the shouts of black warders upholding law and order to silent and orderly assemblies which on the command 'Dismiss' erupted into carnivals of shouts and mad chasings by small boys. Later these carnivals were to be further enlivened by the sounds of cornet, flute, harp, sackbut, psaltery, and dulcimer. Under the Department of Prisons such instruments had been forbidden, no doubt because they could be used as weapons.

That was another thing that held me captive for thirteen years, the transition from the silent parade to the bedlam that followed it. It was almost as though four hundred boys had unanimously decided that in return for the uproarious bedlam they would offer a total silence. In thirteen years it was broken a few times, always by boys of disturbed mind. There was one exception, and that was when a magistrate committed two offenders who had not only been to prison more than once, but who were in their late twenties or their early thirties. They resented bitterly being sent to an institution for boys and made this loudly known during one of the parades. Only my undertaking to ask for a review of their sentences persuaded them to observe the silence. They asked not to be made to sleep in a dormitory, but to be allowed to occupy two of the solitary confinement cells. The problem was solved when they were finally discharged 'from the provisions of the Children's Act'. How the magistrate ever determined that these two had not yet reached the age of twenty we never discovered, but we heard that he had said in passing judgment that, because previous prison sentences had failed, it was time to try a reformatory.

Experiment in Freedom

What was I to do about this unspeakable stench that poured out of every dormitory when the doors were opened at 7.00 a.m.? Could I continue to be the principal of such a 'school' as that?

So, watched by those sixty pairs of eyes, I decided not to lock the dormitories at night, so that boys could visit the lavatories when the need arose. I also decided that all the dormitories would not be opened at once, but that they would be opened at the rate of one each week.

The first three weeks were not anxious ones. Out of four hundred boys, one hundred were children. The youngest was nine. A boy could commit a crime at the age of seven, but we had no seven- or eight-year-olds. The offences of these children were trivial. They should never have been there at all. They had pilfered from shops and fruit stalls and at the markets. One of them had been so foolish as to steal a tin of jam from the pantry of the magistrate's wife. Most of them were children in need of care, but what was to be done with them? There were no industrial schools for black boys, no orphanages, no hostels.

These hundred small boys had a humanising effect on this grim place. Some of them if I came near them on the parade would be conscious that the great *meneer* had taken notice of their existence. Sometimes I would stand still by one of them, usually one of the very smallest. Sometimes I would tweak his ear, and he would give me a brief smile of acknowledgement and frown with still greater concentration. It was as though I had tweaked the ear of the whole reformatory. These were the irrefutable proofs that the aim of the reformatory was not punitive. But quite apart from that, they were to many the only signs of affection they had ever known.

Would these small boys run away from me? It seemed unlikely.

Then why not open up their rooms? They were almost without exception docile and obedient, and eager to please the emperor of their domain. They occupied three of the dormitories, and these were opened on the second, third and fourth Mondays respectively of my principalship. When all the other dormitories were locked at 7.00 p.m. these small boys would rush round and round the interior space which was called the Yard, whistling and yelling and skylarking, delirious with their freedom, until the first and second silence bells rang at 9.00 p.m. and 9.05 p.m. It was my intuition – perhaps not very well founded – that three hundred and forty other boys, listening to this tumult, were looking to the day when they too would be free, but I knew that some of my sixty men looked with fear to it, when this same freedom would be given to boys who had robbed with violence, and had grievously assaulted, and had raped and murdered, many of them not boys at all, but young men, made hard and tough by the life and ways of Kliptown and Pimville and Orlando and Sophiatown, young men who could bludgeon watchmen and scale walls and kill those who stood in their way. And if a dozen of them ganged up together, and murdered the officers on night duty and took their keys and went out into the dark countryside to rob and kill, well, the possibility was terrible to contemplate, but it had to be contemplated. There was only one way in which to guard against such a possibility, and that was to create a strong arm of law and order inside the reformatory itself.

I had come to Diepkloof believing that freedom was the supreme reformatory instrument, yet most of white South Africa believed that a reformatory was a place to which you sent troublemakers to get them out of the way for a while. *Freedom* was a sweet word, hallowed through the ages. But *escaping* or *absconding* were harsh words and they could bring a man's career to an end. If a boy absconded from Diepkloof and murdered a white woman in Comptonville, that would be bad enough. But if he absconded because he had been granted a measure of physical freedom under this new dispensation, that could be the end of me. My colleague Z. went to Houtpoort Reformatory, and under his new dispensation two boys broke into the school armoury, stole a gun, and killed a white storekeeper who resisted their entry. The effect of this on Z. himself was disastrous, for he also had believed that freedom was the supreme reformatory instrument. He had to take long leave, and at the end of it a generous department sent him to an easier job.

It was easy to open five dormitories of small boys who had stolen sweets and fruit and bicycles, many of whom had frequented the markets of Pretoria and Johannesburg and Durban and Bloemfontein trying to make both an honest and a dishonest penny. Like small boys in their circumstances in any part of the world, they were as smart as monkeys, full of tricks, plausible, and some of them very attractive. Yet if left alone, most of them would graduate further in the university of crime, passing on from petty theft to breaking in and robbery, and some of these would finally commit murder, not the honest murder of passion, but the worst crime of all, murder for material gain, usually of some person unknown except as the possessor of desired goods. And even worse no doubt the murder of some person well known, even a father or a mother.

One thing was certain. One could not open five dormitories of small boys and hope to stop at that. After that the opening of the dormitories depended no longer on age, because it was only the young who had been separated from the rest. Therefore from now on I would be giving the freedom of the Yard to boys and young men, some of whom were experienced in breaking in and therefore might not hesitate to try their hands at breaking out, some of whom indeed might not hesitate to attack or kill an unarmed night supervisor who stood between them and freedom. The Yard was by no means absolutely secure against breaking out. It was reasonably so, because the Prisons Department tried to foresee every such eventuality. But if the night supervisors had been overpowered, it would have been possible for determined boys either to seize from them the keys of the main gate, or with the assistance of one's mates to scale the walls. This would have been a self-sacrificing act on the part of those lower down, for they themselves would not have been able to escape. In any event the successful ones would have had to surmount the obstacle of the thirteen-foot barbed wire fence, inclined inwards to make climbing almost impossible. It was the final precaution to keep wire cutters and such tools in a special cupboard which could not be locked at four o'clock until every item was hanging in its place.

Some of the staff members wanted a siren installed, but I resisted it strongly, and decided to stick to the police whistles. I was sure that the sounding of a siren would itself create a kind of feverish situation, with unforeseen consequences. It was also a matter of pride, for if we were in difficulties, I would not want the people of Comptonville to know about it. The sensitiveness of the reforming principal to public opinion is a recurrent theme in reformatory literature. What was more, there were members of the white staff who would not have hesitated to take tales to Comptonville.

I well remember the day when we first discussed the possibility of parading the whole reformatory outside the security of the barbed wire fence. Head Teacher Moloi and Chief Supervisor Stewart-Dunkley were not opposed, but were prepared to leave it to me. So I decided, not without some twinges of anxiety, to hold a parade on the open ground in front of the main building. We invited Major Maynard Page, Chief Magistrate of Johannesburg and Chairman of the Diepkloof Reformatory Board of Management, to be the guest of honour and to take the salute. I explained to the boys the significance and dignity of such an occasion, but did not mention the twinges of anxiety. Four hundred boys marched out, and four hundred boys marched in. It was another step forward, and we all knew it.

It was with greater confidence that we opened the sixth dormitory, and then the seventh, and then the eighth. On the ninth Monday of my principalship eight dormitories were open.

Now at night one hundred and sixty boys were free till 9.00 p.m., to run about the Yard shouting and singing, to form their choirs and bands, and to paint pictures on the whitewashed walls of their open dormitories, pictures such as I have never seen before. There were pictures of boys with stolen handbags fleeing from the cops, of planes and cars and trains, of the streets of Johannesburg both rich and poor, of courts of justice with august magistrates on the bench and naughty boys in the dock. Some boy from Durban would paint a nostalgic picture of the ocean, and a boy homesick for the country would paint an idyllic picture of cows and horses and birds, in a meadow under a willow, weeping into some river of home.

Some of the staff disapproved of this freedom and this activity. Some were honestly afraid of it. If things went wrong, think how badly they could go wrong, with one hundred and sixty boys enjoying the freedom of the Yard, and three unarmed men on night duty, carrying, not weapons of defence, but the keys of the main gates and the doors of twelve yet unopened rooms, containing two hundred and forty boys who were in general tougher and more mature than those already freed. To these doubters on the staff, this freedom and these choirs and this liberty to paint pictures on the walls were bribes and sops, and their acceptance depended upon the whims of boys who had already shown themselves to be wayward and inconstant. But to me these new things were the signs of the beginning of a new order, where life would not be kept under lock and key but liberated under discipline, under the discipline not only of the laws, but of the new selves that would burgeon when they were made free to paint and sing and shout, and to decide whether or not they would begin to live in obedience to the laws.

I was fortunate that at least half of my staff saw these new freedoms, not as bribes, but as the beginning of a new order, dangerous to bring about, but, if it could be brought about, constructive and healing. Gradually the appellation *die tronk* (the jail) fell into disuse and was replaced by *die skool* (the school). The Department itself took similar action, and the warders now became supervisors, while the inmates became pupils. I, who had come as Warden, now became the Principal.

Another thing had already happened that lightened the heavy and sullen atmosphere of Diepkloof. On the first Thursday of my principalship I came back to my office after lunch to find half of the reformatory lined up outside my office, and I said to Captain Stewart-Dunkley, formerly of Poona, and then Chief Warder of Diepkloof, 'What's all this about?' He replied in his impassive military manner, 'Thursday afternoon, sir, is Offences Day.' I said in astonishment, 'But what have they all been up to?' He replied, 'Most of them, sir, have been smoking.'

The Secretary for Education at that time was Professor M. C. Botha, the son of poor parents, yet destined to become one of the most distinguished of South Africa's public servants. He was my boss, and no man ever had a better. He had told me that he was there to help me in what would be no easy task. I went into my office, and telephoned him. I told him that half the reformatory was lined up outside my office, and this was apparently a weekly affair, and that most of them had been caught smoking. Professor Botha said to me, 'You can issue tobacco tomorrow.' I went out to my Chief Warder and said, 'Tobacco will be issued tomorrow,' to which he replied in his impassive manner, 'Very good, sir,' and marched off all the smokers, leaving me with a handful of boys charged with more serious matters, such as smoking the weed called *dagga* or *insangu* (called in America marijuana), committing some assault and so forth.

The announcement at evensong that tobacco would be issued to all boys of sixteen and over, and a ration of sweets to all boys under sixteen, was greeted with something very like cheering, only muted, because such a demonstration was unprecedented.

When I said goodnight and the boys went to their rooms to be counted, I was aware that something had changed somewhere, perhaps only in myself. It seemed to me that many of the boys looked at us out of new eyes, almost as though they were astonished to find that we were human. For the first time I began to feel that my hope would be confirmed, that amongst these four hundred young offenders there was a willingness to give a reasonable obedience to a reasonable authority.

That day also had lasting consequences for myself. After that I never again smoked in working hours.

That was the beginning of our Diepkloof life, thirteen years of disappointment and achievement, of failure and success, of happiness and fulfilment, and of labours prodigious and now almost unbelievable, and an ever-deepening love of an institution and its four hundred wayward boys.

It later grew to five hundred, six hundred, seven hundred, and some people said in all seriousness that the Education Department's policies were making reformatories more attractive, and that boys were committing crimes in order to get into them.

We were to spend at Diepkloof thirteen of the happiest years of our life. I am reminded today of what Francis of Assisi wrote in his will:

'The Lord himself led me amongst them, and I showed mercy to them, and when I left them, what had seemed bitter to me was changed into sweetness of body and soul.'

Final Transformations

When I went to the reformatory block [the morning after a long weekend in Pietermaritzburg] my vice-principal met me with a solemn face, and told me that he had closed all the open dormitories while I was away. He said that he had not felt able to bear the responsibility of having one hundred and sixty boys free in the Yard.

Was he giving me notice that he could not support my policies? Or was he, after half a lifetime spent in the Prison Service, with its discipline and its rigidity, unable to adapt himself to this programme of change and experimentation? Or was he just plain afraid? I think the last was true, so I did not reproach him. Instead I took a step which in retrospect seems to me to have been extraordinary. I gave orders that every dormitory should be opened that night.

I spent the first part of that evening in the Yard, amidst a noise indescribable, of laughter, shouting, home-made music, singing. Several times I made a round of the Yard, being greeted with the Afrikaans '*Goeie naand, meneer*'. At nine o'clock the first silence bell was rung, and four hundred boys went to their rooms. At five minutes past nine the second bell was rung, and the silence was absolute.

As I write these words, I find my eyes are wet. Why did it happen that way? I just don't know. How was I to know that four hundred boys, of whom at least a hundred would become the hardened occupants of prisons, and some of whom had no regard for human life at all, would in return for this gift of an open dormitory observe this total silence? It was a popular reformatory theory of course, that if you treat prisoners well, they'll treat you well too. But it was a theory pooh-poohed by all the realists; the only thing to do with a prisoner was to trust him no further than you could throw him.

One of the results of the opening of the dormitories and the removal of the buckets was that the reformatory latrines could not cope with the new demands. The department came to my aid. I was to be allowed to build a bucket latrine with eight units. Within the week the contractor was there and we decided to build the latrine in the rear exit passage shown on the plan as L–L. Hardly had the contractor left the reformatory when another arrived with an order to build a latrine with eight units. We decided to build this second latrine onto the first and now had a magnificent latrine with sixteen units. The second contractor had hardly gone when the PWD inspector arrived.

'Who gave you permission to build a second latrine?'

'Nobody. The second contractor told me he had been instructed to build a latrine.'

'Why didn't you stop him?'

'You must understand', I said, 'that I have no authority to interfere with contractors.'

I was later reproved, but meanwhile we had acquired a brand-new set of latrines which were kept spotless. This had one important consequence. Typhoid fever, which had been the scourge of the reformatory and the cause of many deaths, almost completely disappeared.

Freedom within custodial walls isn't the real thing. How could one introduce freedom outside them? This was the question that now exercised my mind. For I clung to the belief – which was at that time founded on faith – that you could not cultivate a sense of purpose and responsibility unless it were accompanied by physical freedom, and that the granting of physical freedom would prove far less dangerous than one feared.

There was one great asset – another piece of luck – and that was that we had a farm of nine hundred acres. Some prisons and reformatory schools have no land but that on which they are built. For them the problem of freedom outside the custodial walls is difficult indeed.

My first plan was not a good one. It was to invite all the supervisors to pick from their *spans* those boys who would be unlikely to abuse such a freedom. This freedom they would be given with due ceremony at evensong. Each boy would be given a shirt the pocket of which had been covered with a piece of green cloth. This green pocket soon became known as the *vakasha* badge, the word *vakasha* (pronounced *va-ga'-sha*), meaning in Zulu 'to go for a walk'.

On Fridays at evensong these chosen boys would be paraded before the whole congregation, and facing me. As the names were called out, each boy in turn would come and stand in front of me. I would say to him, 'Today you are receiving your *vakasha* badge. What do you have to say?' The boy would then turn to face the congregation and say:

'Today I receive my *vakasha* badge.
I promise not to go beyond the boundaries of the farm.
I promise not to touch anything that is not mine.
I promise to obey the rules of the school.'

He would then turn to me again and be given a shirt with the green badge. When all the badges had been given, I would say to the congregation, 'Today these boys you see before you have received the *vakasha* badge,' and the congregation would applaud.

The *vakasha* badge now enabled supervisors to use the free boys as messengers, or to allow them to work apart from the main *span*. But the big privilege was to be signed out at the gate at two o'clock on a Sunday afternoon, to have the freedom of the farm, and to return to the gate at fifteen minutes to five. On the first *vakasha* afternoon, some fifty boys were signed out and the same number were signed in. The actual signing out was a great event for the whole reformatory, and a large crowd gathered to watch the lucky ones go out.

But the plan did not work out as well as I had hoped. Some boys who had been picked out by their supervisors as trustworthy used the *vakasha* badge to abscond. Its weakness was further exposed by a boy who absconded without the *vakasha* badge, and the only way to do that was to make a sudden bolt for freedom. He was apprehended and brought back, and when asked why he had absconded, he gave the answer: 'You gave Johannes the badge and he had been here only a month; I have been here for a year and have behaved myself, but you gave me nothing. So I ran away.'

I had in fact failed to realise the importance of *time* to those who have been deprived of freedom. Time is the overriding interest of their lives. In strict prisons the granting of privileges, the right to send a letter, even the issue of a spoon of jam, all depend on time.

The boy who had absconded because I gave him nothing brought about a big change in the free plan. From then on behaviour was not the sole criterion; the two criteria were now *behaviour* and *time*. The time was fixed at nine months, and after that period any boy whose behaviour had been good would receive the *vakasha* badge.

The second plan was a decided improvement on the first. The boy who had already done nine months of his reformatory term was less likely to abscond than the boy who had done one or two months. Further, the fact that the free badge would in all likelihood be granted after nine months meant that the urge to make a bolt for it before that time was lessened. The absconding rate *after* freedom settled into a steady pattern that was to be consistent for thirteen years. Of every hundred boys receiving the badge, *one* would abscond on the first occasion that he was signed out at the gate, *one* would abscond within the next four weeks, *one* would abscond at some later date, sometimes when his reformatory term was almost completed. *Ninety-seven* boys would not abscond at all.

Why was that? Why should a promise prove so binding on the delinquent population of the slums and the markets of South Africa? I do not know the answer to that question. It was again a part of my luck, for if it had turned out otherwise, even perhaps disastrous, I would have had to return to freedom within the custodial walls.

But whatever the right answer was, a very epigrammatic one was given by a boy who had been a determined absconder until he received his freedom. 'When I made my promise,' he said, 'it was like a chain on my leg.' And for many it was undoubtedly true. The most extraordinary example was that of a boy who after receiving his freedom absconded and made his way to Durban 450 miles away. He then gave himself up to the police. 'Why did you do that?' I asked. 'Because of my promise,' he said.

Absconding under the prisons regime was in fact common. It involved a sudden break from the *span*, except in the isolated cases of 'trusties', who could abscond with ease, but there were few of these. Before my arrival absconding had been at the rate of thirteen per month. When an abscondment occurred all the *spans* were recalled to the main block, and members of the staff were thus enabled to join in the pursuit. It was of course my ambition to bring this number down.

When an absconder was returned to the reformatory, he was

greeted with howls of execration, and was assaulted, sometimes severely. The boys of the reformatory held the belief – or acted as though they held the belief – that each time a boy absconded the discipline became harsher. How the discipline became progressively harsher thirteen times in one month I could never discover. Among those joining most heartily in the assault could well be some boy who would abscond the day following. After the reformatory had dealt with him, the boy would be officially punished by the warden, and would be made to wear a red shirt till further notice.

After one severe assault, the chief culprits were brought to me, and the conversation went something like this.

SELF: Why did you assault this boy?
BOY: Because he ran away.
SELF: I believe you ran away yourself once.
BOY *(a trifle disconcerted)*: That was two months ago.
SELF: What has it to do with you that this boy ran away?
BOY *(now sure of his ground)*: He makes it harder for us.
SELF: In what way will it be harder?
BOY: It will be harder.
SELF *(to the others)*: Do you all agree?
OTHERS: We all agree.

Under the Prisons Department these assaults had been winked at. They were certainly regarded as useful curbs on absconding. But now they were to be no more. The red shirts were also withdrawn and were used to make pocket badges for a new breed, the *headboys*, who were appointed to be in charge of the open dormitories. The twenty rooms were divided into four houses, each in charge of a *house-captain*. At the head of the hierarchy was the *senior*, who was inevitably a young man rather than a boy. The new head-boy was also brought before the congregation, and made appropriate promises, after which he received his badge and a round of applause.

I could not foresee in 1935 that the consequence of increasing the amount of physical freedom would be to reduce absconding drastically, to change the atmosphere of the reformatory from one of grimness to one of industrious gaiety, and almost to eliminate the feelings of anxiety and tension. I was too deeply committed to see that the setbacks were only falterings in a ceaseless moving forward. I passed through periods of despair, and said (rather than prayed) to

DIEPKLOOF REFORMATORY BEFORE
FRONT PORTION OF SECURITY FENCE WAS REMOVED

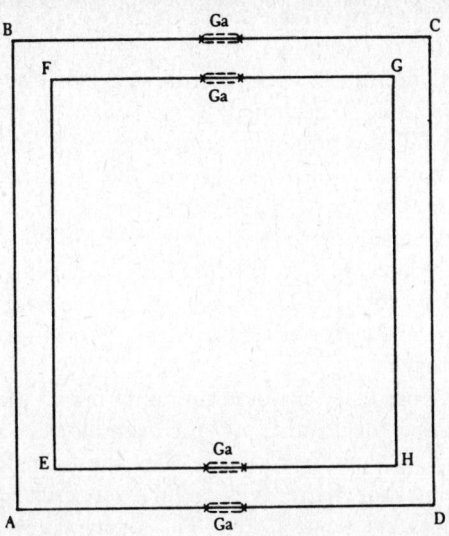

DIEPKLOOF REFORMATORY
FRONT PORTION OF SECURITY FENCE REMOVED

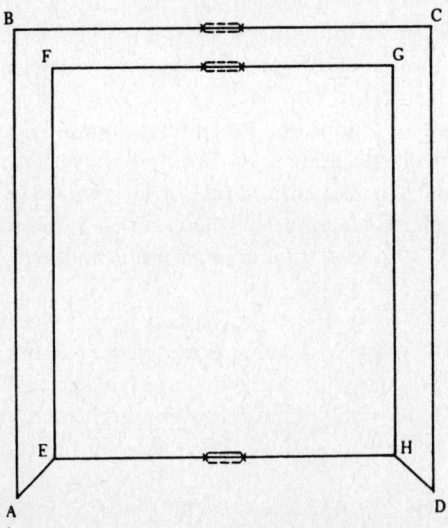

God, 'Don't You want this to happen? Because if You don't want it to happen, I'm going back to a safer job.'

But apparently He did want it to happen.

So the first six months at Diepkloof drew to their end. The atmosphere was changing. The closed dormitories were no longer there to reproach us. The morning stench had gone. Typhoid fever was going. Small boys did not any longer tremble when one approached them. The clean whitewashed walls were no longer sacrosanct; pictures could be painted on the dormitory walls.

But how could one boast of all this, and to what extent was it real, while the main block stood behind its thirteen-foot barbed wire fence, inclining inwards, so that it was impossible to scale? That was the next step to take.

The barbed wire fence enclosed the entire main block, as shown, ABCD being the fence, and EFGH the main block. Ga, Ga, Ga, Ga are the gates. On New Year's Day, 1936, the front fence AD was taken down, and short fences AE and DH were erected.

At first it was like being naked. The great main gate was taken down, and the administrative offices, including my own, were now open to the world. Mr H. C. Fick, known to all, boys and staff, as Oubaas, a man of about forty, was now put in charge of all the gardens that were to be. His first job was to make a garden where the fence AD had been. Prominent in his first garden were geraniums, and I became known as 'The man who pulled up the barbed wire and planted geraniums', although it was only half my doing.

The establishment of the gardens was the first attempt to diversify the occupations of the reformatory. Oubaas Fick was given five supervisors and a hundred boys. He was a kind of genius. All our roads were lined with gum trees, but now they all came down and were replaced by ornamental trees set in lawns. He established a nursery, and raised seedlings of many kinds. It became one of my greatest pleasures to visit it on my inspection rounds.

On New Year's Day, 1937, the barbed wire fence was removed entirely and the massive iron supports were torn out of their concrete. The reformatory block seemed more naked than ever, but the feeling of apprehension was largely absent. The announcement that the fence was to be removed was greeted with shouts and applause.

Final Transformations

In 1938 the whole character of the reformatory changed, and the main block ceased to be the main centre of the reformatory. The Public Works Department built on an open piece of land below the main block four free hostels, each to accommodate twenty-five boys. Each hostel consisted of a cottage with rooms for an African teacher and his wife, and a communal dining room for the twenty-five boys.

Arranged in a semicircle around the cottage were five huts or *rondavels*, each housing five boys. These were boys who had used their freedom well, and they were now allowed home leave once a month. Of every hundred who were allowed this leave, one would

THE FIRST FOUR FREE HOSTELS

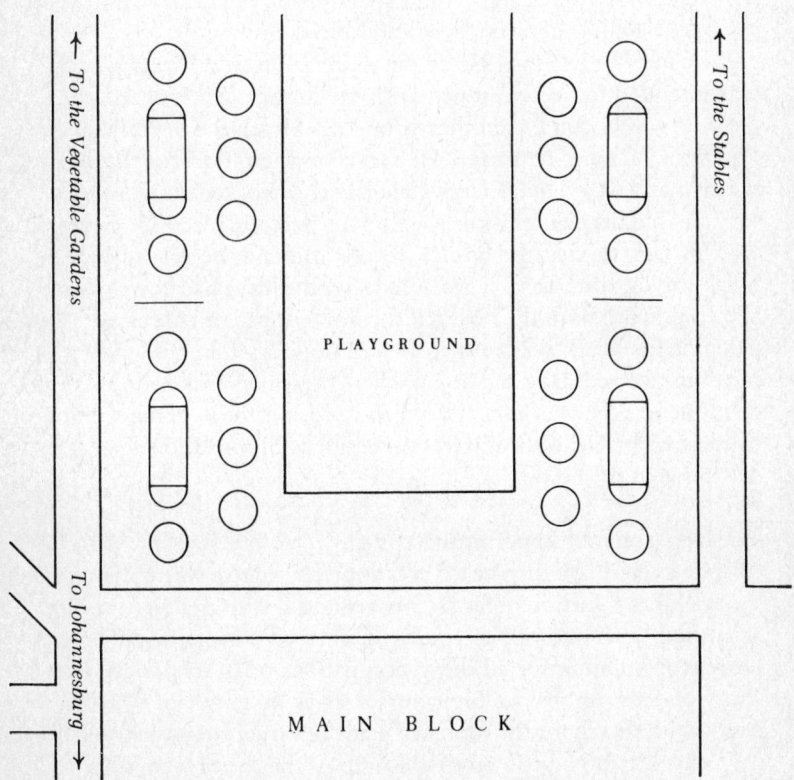

not return, one would return late, one would return under the influence of liquor. Ninety-seven returned, prompt and sober. The absconding rate, which [before these changes] had been eleven per month, dropped steadily year by year, and when we left it stood at three per month.

I left Diepkloof in 1948, and the final step of its transformation was taken in that year, when the department agreed to build in Orlando, the great African township and the forerunner of Soweto, a hostel for twenty Diepkloof boys. Here, after having spent nine months in the main block, having survived the temptations of the *vakasha* badge and the home leave, and after having lived for six months or more in a free hostel, a Johannesburg boy would be allowed to spend his last six months in a working hostel, where he could work under our supervision and learn to earn, spend, and perhaps save money. If it worked well, other hostels would follow.

We had as far back as 1936 begun a kind of aftercare section, which was intended to keep in touch with the homes of all Johannesburg boys. It was begun by another young man from the Special Service Battalion, 'Lanky' de Lange. He served as the model for the young white man in *Cry, the Beloved Country* who worked at the reformatory and hid his gentler nature behind the fierce and frowning eyes. It was his task to visit the homes, to recommend the granting of the home leaves, often to visit the home after the leave had been granted, and to prepare both the boy and the home for the final release. The value of his work was immense, and he was often able to restore relations between boy and home where these had broken down. The delinquent boy was not always the product of a derelict home; sometimes his delinquency was the result of his rebellion against the discipline of the home.

The Department had permitted a drastic reform in my first year. Up till then every boy when he left was apprenticed to a white farmer for the unexpired portion of his retention period. This practice was now abolished, and one of the results of this was the introduction of workshop training for all those occupations open to African boys. Most of these shops we built ourselves at first, out of wattle and daub, with thatch for the roof. We made our own shoes, tailored our own clothes, did our own tin-smithing. Other boys were trained in building and laundry work. About one hundred boys still worked on the farm, mostly those from rural and agricultural areas, and another hundred were trained in nursery work and horticulture. The gardens of Diepkloof became known for their beauty.

Our Farm Manager watched with dismay the diversification of the educational programme of the reformatory. With a few exceptions all the boys had been under his control, but now he lost all the small boys, of whom there were about one hundred. They were sent permanently to school, and that meant the appointment of three new black teachers, and, incidentally, the removal of the two sentry boxes.

These hundred small boys formed the *Kleinspan*, and in the afternoons they played and did small chores, such as weeding and wood carrying. They were put under the supervision of one of the older boys at the school, Daniel Bob. His nickname was Majohnnie, and he was another genius. He stood less than five feet, and was never to grow any taller, but his discipline was perfect, and his understanding of small boys profound.

When the time came for him to leave the reformatory he came to see me.

'*Meneer*, I do not want to go back to Kimberley.'

'Why not, Majohnnie?'

'Because I shall be back here in a month.'

'Why should that be?'

'*Meneer*, I know Kimberley and I know myself. I shall be back in a month.'

'Then what must I do?'

'*Meneer* must employ me here to look after the *Kleinspan*.' So I asked the department to allow me to employ four reformatory boys as supervisors after their discharge. This in fact was in line with its own policy of appealing to employers to give a chance to boys and girls released from reformatories and industrial schools, and it would have been difficult to refuse me. Of these four, Majohnnie was an outstanding success, and remained so all his life. Why a delinquent boy from a derelict home should have come to cherish, almost fiercely, such qualities as punctuality, reliability, loyalty, and honesty I do not claim to understand. After I left Diepkloof he married, and had seven children, with whose education I helped him. In almost every letter he wrote he told me that his committal to the reformatory was the luckiest event of his life, and that he was trying to teach his children the lessons that the reformatory had taught him.

Not all were impressed by this change. One of our critics was Dr Hendrik Verwoerd, then editor of *Die Transvaler*, who described Diepkloof as the place where one said 'Please and thank you to the black misters', and dismissed the educational programme, the system of increasing responsibility and freedom as *vertroeteling* (pampering). When he became Minister of Native Affairs, he had the responsibility for African boys transferred to himself, and closed down Diepkloof altogether, and transferred its boys to different parts of South Africa, according to their ethnic grouping, where the practice of working for white farmers was re-introduced.

Many people asked me if this did not break my heart. No, it did not. What would have broken my heart would have been to have had to stay there, under a Minister with whom I had almost nothing in common. He would have discharged me or removed me, and perhaps have embittered my life. For this I have to thank that strange event, the writing of a book which captured the hearts of so many of the people of the world.

The thirtieth day of June 1948 was my last day at Diepkloof Reformatory. I attended to this and that, but in fact I had already withdrawn. I sat at my office table and suddenly the enormity of my action came home to me. Before I knew what had happened I had broken into a fit of desperate sobbing. I tried to control it but was unable to do so.

So we left Diepkloof, you weeping, and I, shut up in my office sobbing for the first time since my childhood days. So ended those thirteen years.

Ha'penny

Of the six hundred boys at the reformatory, about one hundred were from ten to fourteen years of age. My Department had from time to time expressed the intention of taking them away, and of establishing a special institution for them, more like an industrial school than a reformatory.

This would have been a good thing, for their offences were very trivial, and they would have been better by themselves. Had such a school been established, I should have liked to be Principal of it myself, for it would have been an easier job; small boys turn instinctively towards affection, and one controls them by it, naturally and easily.

Some of them, if I came near them, either on parade or in school or at football, would observe me watchfully, not directly or fully, but obliquely and secretly; sometimes I would surprise them at it, and make some small sign of recognition, which would satisfy them so that they would cease to observe me, and would give their full attention to the event of the moment. But I knew that my authority was thus confirmed and strengthened.

The secret relations with them were a source of continuous pleasure to me. Had they been my own children I would no doubt have given a greater expression to it. But often I would move through the silent and orderly parade, and stand by one of them. He would look straight in front of him with a little frown of concentration that expressed both childish awareness of and manly indifference to my nearness. Sometimes I would tweak his ear, and he would give me a brief smile of acknowledgement, or frown with still greater concentration. It was natural, I suppose, to confine these outward expressions to the very smallest, but they were taken as symbolic, and some older boys would observe them and take themselves to be included. It was a relief, when the reformatory was passing through times of turbulence and trouble, and when there was danger of estrangement between authority and boys, to make these simple and natural gestures, which were reassurances to both me and them that nothing important had changed.

On Sunday afternoons when I was on duty I would take my car to the reformatory and watch the free boys being signed out at the gate. This simple operation was also watched by many boys not free, who would tell each other, 'In so many weeks I'll be signed out myself.' Among the watchers were always some of the small boys, and these I would take by turns in the car. We would go out to the Potchefstroom Road with its ceaseless stream of traffic, and to the Baragwanath crossroads, and come back by the Van Wyksrus road to the reformatory. I would talk to them about their families, their parents, their sisters and brothers, and I would pretend to know nothing of Durban, Port Elizabeth, Potchefstroom, and Clocolan, and ask them if these places were bigger than Johannesburg.

One of the small boys was Ha'penny, and he was about twelve years old. He came from Bloemfontein and was the biggest talker of them all. His mother worked in a white person's house, and he had two brothers and two sisters. His brothers were Richard and Dickie, and his sisters Anna and Mina.

'Richard and Dickie?' I asked.

'Yes, *meneer*.'

'In English,' I said, 'Richard and Dickie are the same name.'

When we returned to the reformatory, I sent for Ha'penny's papers; there it was plainly set down, Ha'penny was a waif, with no relatives at all. He had been taken in from one home to another, but he was naughty and uncontrollable, and eventually had taken to pilfering at the market.

I then sent for the Letter Book, and found that Ha'penny wrote regularly, or rather that others wrote for him till he could write himself, to Mrs Betty Maarman, of 48 Vlak Street, Bloemfontein. But Mrs Maarman had never once replied to him. When questioned, he had said, 'Perhaps she is sick.' I sat down and wrote at once to the Social Welfare Officer at Bloemfontein, asking him to investigate.

The next time I had Ha'penny out in the car I questioned him again about his family. And he told me the same as before, his mother, Richard and Dickie, Anna and Mina. But he softened the 'D' of

Dickie, so that it sounded now like Tickie.

'I thought you said Dickie,' I said.

'I said Tickie,' he said.

He watched me with concealed apprehension, and I came to the conclusion that this waif of Bloemfontein was a clever boy, who had told me a story that was all imagination, and had changed one single letter of it to make it safe from any question. And I thought I understood it all too, that he was ashamed of being without a family and had invented them all, so that no one might discover that he was fatherless and motherless and that no one in the world cared whether he was alive or dead. This gave me a strong feeling for him, and I went out of my way to manifest towards him that fatherly care that the State, though not in those words, had enjoined upon me by giving me this job.

Then the letter came from the Social Welfare Officer in Bloemfontein, saying that Mrs Betty Maarman of 48 Vlak Street was a real person, and that she had four children, Richard and Dickie, Anna and Mina, but that Ha'penny was no child of hers, and she knew him only as a derelict of the streets. She had never answered his letters, because he wrote to her as 'Mother', and she was no mother of his, nor did she wish to play any such role. She was a decent woman, a faithful member of the church, and she had no thought of corrupting her family by letting them have anything to do with such a child.

But Ha'penny seemed to me anything but the usual delinquent; his desire to have a family was so strong, and his reformatory record was so blameless, and his anxiety to please and obey so great, that I began to feel a great duty towards him. Therefore I asked him about his 'mother'.

He could not speak enough of her, or with too high praise. She was loving, honest, and strict. Her home was clean. She had affection for all her children. It was clear that the homeless child, even as he had attached himself to me, would have attached himself to her; he had observed her even as he had observed me, but did not know the secret of how to open her heart, so that she would take him in, and save him from the lonely life that he led.

'Why did you steal when you had such a mother?' I asked.

He could not answer that; not all his brains nor his courage could find an answer to such a question, for he knew that with such a mother he would not have stolen at all.

'The boy's name is Dickie,' I said, 'not Tickie.'

And then he knew the deception was revealed. Another boy might have said, 'I told you it was Dickie,' but he was too intelligent for that; he knew that if I had established that the boy's name was Dickie, I must have established other things too. I was shocked by the immediate and visible effect of my action. His whole brave assurance died within him, and he stood there exposed, not as a liar, but as a homeless child who had surrounded himself with mother, brothers, and sisters, who did not exist. I had shattered the very foundations of his pride, and his sense of human significance.

He fell sick at once, and the doctor said it was tuberculosis. I wrote at once to Mrs Maarman, telling her the whole story, of how this small boy had observed her, and had decided that she was the person he desired for his mother. But she wrote back saying that she could take no responsibility for him. For one thing, Ha'penny was a Mosuto, and she was a coloured woman; for another, she had never had a child in trouble, and how could she take such a boy?

Tuberculosis is a strange thing; sometimes it manifests itself suddenly in the most unlikely host, and swiftly sweeps to the end. Ha'penny withdrew himself from the world, from all Principals and mothers, and the doctor said there was little hope. In desperation I sent money for Mrs Maarman to come.

She was a decent, homely woman, and seeing that the situation was serious, she, without fuss or embarrassment, adopted Ha'penny for her own. The whole reformatory accepted her as his mother. She sat the whole day with him, and talked to him of Richard and Dickie, Anna and Mina, and how they were all waiting for him to come home. She poured out her affection on him, and had no fear of his sickness, nor did she allow it to prevent her from satisfying his hunger to be owned. She talked to him of what they would do when he came back, and how he would go to the school and what they would buy for Guy Fawkes night.

He in his turn gave his whole attention to her, and when I visited him he was grateful, but I had passed out of his world. I felt judged in that I had sensed only the existence and not the measure of his desire. I wished I had done something sooner, more wise, more prodigal.

We buried him on the reformatory farm, and Mrs Maarman said to me, 'When you put up the cross, put he was my son.'

'I'm ashamed,' she said, 'that I wouldn't take him.'

'The sickness,' I said, 'the sickness would have come.'

'No,' she said, shaking her head with certainty. 'It wouldn't have come. And if it had come at home, it would have been different.'

So she left for Bloemfontein, after her strange visit to a reformatory. And I was left too, with the resolve to be more prodigal in the task that the State, though not in so many words, had enjoined on me.

The Divided House

Of all the boys at the reformatory, Jacky was one of the strangest.

He had once been a Pondo of Pondoland, but the big city was now in his blood. He was a closed-up, reserved kind of boy, and had no close companions; but he enjoyed a kind of popularity none the less, for he played a magnificent game of football. We gave him his freedom because no one knew much about him, not even the Tailoring Instructor who had worked with him for months. Of every hundred boys we made free, three absconded at once, the first time they were allowed to roam about the farm on their own. But another three had a conscience, and absconded only on the second or fifth or seventh occasion. Jacky was one of these, and one Sunday afternoon he failed to report back at five o'clock.

Some days after, I was visiting some boys who had been temporarily transferred to the non-European hospital, and whom should I see in one of the wards, with an African constable sitting guard over him, but Jacky. I told the constable he was one of my boys, and asked if I might speak to him.

'What are you doing here, Jacky?'

He looked at me shamefacedly.

'I was shot, father,' he said.

'How did you get shot?'

'I was breaking into a house, father.'

Of course Jacky lost his freedom when the magistrate returned him to the reformatory, and he went back to the main building. But he was such a good tailor that he was allowed to return to his old work. When he had been back for a short time, he asked to see me, and the Tailoring Instructor brought him in.

'Jacky has a story to tell the Principal,' he said, and then he looked at me apologetically. 'It's a strange story,' he said.

'Well, Jacky?'

'When I was in hospital, father, a voice spoke to me.'

'A voice? What voice?'

'God's voice, father.'

'And what did He say?'

'He said, "Jacky, you won't die, your work is not yet finished." '

'And what did you say?'

'I said, "Father, what is the work?" '

'Yes?'

'And He said, "Jacky, I want you to be a priest." '

I sat and considered it, and then I said to him, 'That's a new kind of work for you.'

If there was any irony, he took no notice.

'It's a new kind of work,' he said.

'How far have you been in school, Jacky?'

'Standard Four, father.'

'A priest has to go further than that.'

'I'm ready,' he said.

'You're asking', I said, 'to go to the school?'

'Yes, father.'

'Then you can go to the school.'

So Jacky was put in Standard Five in the school, and though not brilliant, he worked hard and well.

In a few days he was back with the Head Teacher.

'What is it, Jacky?'

'Father, I am asking to go back to the free hostels.'

'Absconders don't go back to the free hostels,' I said. 'They go back to the main building.'

'I know,' he said, 'but I can't pray and study in the main building. There's too much noise.'

I knew that Jacky was spending much time in prayer and study, when he wasn't playing football.

'You can go back to the hostels,' I said. 'Are you in earnest, Jacky?'

'I'm in earnest, father. I am determined to be a priest.'

So Jacky went back to the hostels. He was an exemplary character, quiet and obedient, and spent much time by himself, praying and reading.

The most extraordinary outward change was in his bodily cleanliness; he looked wholesome, and his face was shining. He washed and ironed his clothes every few days, which was really against the rules. He made more progress in school than his intelligence promised, and asked if he could preach in the hostels, where he had a small band of disciples. There was nothing extreme about it, for he spoke quietly of his own conversion, and asked others to follow his example before it was too late; in the meantime he went on playing his magnificent football. So he continued for some months, and it appeared that some deep change had taken place in his life, and that he thought nothing of the long period of training that stretched out before him, so long as he could become a priest.

Therefore it was a disappointment when he failed one day to appear at the evening parade of all free boys. The Head Teacher brought him to me.

'Why were you not at parade, Jacky?'

'It was the voice,' he said.

'What did it tell you, Jacky?'

'It told me to go and pray, father.'

'Where?'

'Down at the trees by the stables.'

'A priest must obey the laws,' I said.

'I know, father.'

'Therefore,' I said, 'if this voice tells you again to go and pray, you will go at once and ask your teacher's permission.'

'I promise it, father.'

So Jacky continued again for some months, washing and ironing his clothes, working hard at school, playing hard at football, and preaching once a week at the hostels. Then he failed again to appear at the parade.

The Head Teacher sent at once to the trees by the stables, but no Jacky was there.

'Have you thought, sir,' asked the Head Teacher diffidently, 'that he might be smoking *dagga*?'

Now although the smoking of *dagga* is common in our cities, and although it is one of the great reformatory enemies, I was shaken, and said, 'What makes you think that?'

'Sometimes his manner is strange,' he said.

And that of course is the great sign, after the smell of the weed itself; for the humble come out with sudden insolence, and the obedient with sudden disobedience, the open-hearted become secretive, the gay sullen.

The next morning he brought Jacky to me.

'Well, Jacky?'

'Father?'

'Where were you yesterday?'

'In the trees by the stables, father.'

'Praying?'

'Yes, father.'

I looked him in the eyes for some time, but he could not endure it.

'Jacky.'

'Yes, father.'

'We searched in the trees by the stables.'

He did not maintain that we had searched inefficiently, nor did he pretend that he was in some other trees. He watched me anxiously, almost humbly.

'Would you lie to me?' I asked.

And he said in a subdued voice, 'No, father.'

'Have you been smoking *dagga*?'

He winced. The question was a hard blow to him. He would not look at me, but kept his eyes on the ground.

'Answer me, Jacky.'

'I smoked it,' he said.

I was silent a long time, so that he might feel that his admission had shocked me.

'You want to be a priest?'

'Yes, father.'

'You want to be a priest,' I said, 'and you want to smoke *dagga* also.'

My voice rose, and he turned his face away from me.

'But it cannot be done,' I said.

He looked at me with anguish.

'You are forcing me,' I said, 'you are forcing me to take away your freedom and send you to some other job.'

'No, no,' he said. He dropped on his knees in the office and began to pray silently. It was a strange thing to be there. When he was finished, he rose and said to me earnestly, 'I do not want to smoke *dagga*.'

'How many more chances do you want?' I said.

'One, father.'

'You can have it,' I said.

Yet of all reformatory enemies, *dagga* is the most insidious. It tempts free boys to break bounds, and to go seeking it in Pimville, Kliptown, and Orlando. It tempts them to steal goods, especially clothes, which they trade for the terrible weed. And Jacky's next offence was to steal a jacket from one of the hostels, and to sell it in Orlando. So he was brought to me again. But this time it was a Special Court, which we used when we wished to bring home to a boy the gravity of an offence. The Principal and the Vice-Principal were there, and the Chief Supervisor, the African Head Teacher, and the Tailoring Instructor. When Jacky came in, he was shocked to see us all.

He pleaded guilty to the offences of theft and buying *dagga*, so that there was nothing to do but to decide how to deal with him. After the long discussion I said to him, 'The Court does not say you cannot be a priest. But it says you must go back to the Main Building, and lose your freedom, and that you must go back to your tailoring. Yet if you are after some time still determined to be a priest, you will be allowed to return to the hostels and the school.'

Jacky looked at us as though he could not believe it, as though he could not believe in such a punishment. He could not speak, and it was uncomfortable to look at him.

'The football,' said Jacky, hoarsely.

'What about the football, Jacky?'

'Couldn't you take away the football?' he said. 'Couldn't you take the freedom? But not the school, not the school.'

It was painful to listen to him, so I looked at my fellow judges, but, like judges, they were impassive. Left to ourselves, we might have done something; left to myself, I might have done something. But I had asked them to judge, and I could not speak first; and I was the Principal, so perhaps they felt they could not speak first either. So society and the law were not moved. Jacky was taken away, the thief recompensed, the priest defeated.

Shortly afterwards Jacky attacked the head-boy of the Tailor's Shop with a pair of scissors, and escaped into the trees. He was arrested in Pretoria for house-breaking, but this time he was sent to prison for six months. I had a letter from him there, repenting of all past follies, and saying that he was still determined to be a priest. The letter was earnest and penitent, and I had no doubt that the struggle was still being waged; therefore I answered with words of encouragement, telling him that he could come back to us if he wished. Yet I knew that the boy who wrote the letter would, so far as men knew, always be defeated, till one day he would give up both hope and ghost, and leave to his enemy the sole tenancy of the divided house.

Death of a Tsotsi

Abraham Moletisane was his name but no one ever called him anything but Spike. He was a true child of the city, gay, careless, plausible; but for all that, he was easy to manage and anxious to please. He was clean though flashy in his private dress. The khaki shirts and shorts of the reformatory were too drab for him, and he had a red scarf and yellow handkerchief which he arranged to peep out of his shirt pocket. He also had a pair of black-and-white shoes and a small but highly coloured feather in his cap. Now the use of private clothes, except after the day's work, was forbidden; but he wore the red scarf on all occasions, saying, with an earnest expression that changed into an enigmatic smile if you looked too long at him, that his throat was sore. That was a great habit of his, to look away when you talked to him, and to smile at some unseen thing.

He passed through the first stages of the reformatory very successfully. He had two distinct sets of visitors, one his hard-working mother and his younger sister, and the other a group of flashy young men from the city. His mother and the young men never came together, and I think he arranged it so. While we did not welcome his second set of visitors, we did not forbid them so long as they behaved themselves; it was better for us to know about them than otherwise.

One day his mother and sister brought a friend Elizabeth, who was a quiet and clean-looking person like themselves. Spike told me that his mother wished him to marry this girl, but that the girl was very independent, and refused to hear of it unless he reformed and gave up the company of the tsotsis.

'And what do you say, Spike?'

He would not look at me, but tilted his head up and surveyed the ceiling, smiling hard at it, and dropping his eyes but not his head to take an occasional glance at me. I did not know exactly what was in his mind, but it was clear to me that he was beginning to feel confidence in the reformatory.

'It doesn't help to say to her, just O.K., O.K.,' he said. 'She wants it done before everybody, as the Principal gives the first freedom.'

'What do you mean, before everybody?'

'Before my family and hers.'

'And are you willing?'

Spike smiled harder than ever at the ceiling, as though at some secret but delicious joy. Whether it was that he was savouring the delight of deciding his future, I do not know. Or whether he was savouring the delight of keeping guessing two whole families and the reformatory, I do not know either.

He was suddenly serious. 'If I promise her, I'll keep it,' he said. 'But I won't be forced.'

'No one's forcing you,' I said.

He lowered his head and looked at me, as though I did not understand the ways of women.

Although Spike was regarded as a weak character, he met all the temptations of increasing physical freedom very successfully. He went to the free hostels, and after some months there he received the privilege of special week-end leave to go home. He swaggered out, and he swaggered back, punctual to the minute. How he timed it I do not know, for he had no watch; but in all the months that he had privilege, he was never late.

It was just after he had received his first special leave that one of his city friends was sent to the reformatory also. The friend's name was Walter, and within a week of his arrival he and Spike had a fight, and both were sent to me. Walter alleged that Spike had hit him first, and Spike did not deny it.

'Why did you hit him, Spike?'

'He insulted me, *meneer*.'

'How?'

At length he came out with it.

'He said I was reformed.'

We could not help laughing at that, not much of course, for it was clear to me that Spike did not understand our laughter, and that he accepted it only because he knew we were well disposed towards him.

'If I said you were reformed, Spike,' I said, 'would you be insulted?'

'No, *meneer*.'

'Then why did he insult you?'

He thought that it was a difficult question. Then he said, 'He did not mean anything good, *meneer*. He meant I was back to being a child.'

'You are not,' I said. 'You are going forward to being a man.'

He was mollified by that, and I warned him not to fight again. He accepted my rebuke, but he said to me, 'This fellow is out to make trouble for me. He says I must go back to the tsotsis when I come out.'

I said to Walter, 'Did you say that?'

Walter was hurt to the depths and said, 'No, *meneer*.'

When they had gone I sent for de Villiers whose job it is to know every home in Johannesburg that has a boy at the reformatory. It was not an uncommon story, of a decent widow left with a son and daughter. She had managed to control the daughter, but not the son, and Spike had got in with a gang of tsotsis; as a result of one of their exploits he had found himself in court, but had not betrayed his friends. Then he had gone to the reformatory, which apart from anything it did itself, had enabled his mother to regain her hold on him, so that he had now decided to forsake the tsotsis, to get a job through de Villiers, and to marry the girl Elizabeth and live with her in his mother's house.

A week later Spike came to see me again.

'The Principal must forbid these friends of Walter to visit the reformatory,' he said.

'Why, Spike?'

'They are planning trouble for me, *meneer*.'

The boy was no longer smiling, but looked troubled, and I sat considering his request. I called in de Villiers, and we discussed it in Afrikaans, which Spike understood. But we were talking a rather high Afrikaans for him, and his eyes went from one face to the other, trying to follow what we said. If I forbade these boys to visit the reformatory, what help would that be to Spike? Would their resentment against him be any the less? Would they forget it because they did not see him? Might this not be a further cause for resentment against him? After all, one cannot remake the world; one can do all one can in a reformatory, but when the time comes, one has to take away one's hands. It was true that de Villiers would look after him, but such supervision had its defined limits As I looked at the boy's troubled face, I also was full of trouble for him for he had of his choice bound himself with chains, and now, when he wanted of his choice to put them off, he found it was not so easy to do.

He looked at us intently, and I could see that he felt excluded, and wished to be brought in again.

'Did you understand what we said, Spike?'

'Not everything, *meneer*.'

'I am worried about one thing,' I said. 'Which is better for you, to forbid these boys, or not to forbid them?'

'To forbid them,' he said.

'They might say,' I said, '"Now he'll pay for this."'

'The Principal does not understand,' he said. 'My time is almost finished at the reformatory. I don't want trouble before I leave.'

'I'm not worried about trouble here,' I said. 'I'm worried about trouble outside.'

He looked at me anxiously, as though I had not fully grasped the matter.

'I'm not worried about here,' I said with asperity. 'I can look after you here. If someone tried to make trouble, do you think I can't find the truth?'

He did not wish to doubt my ability, but he remained anxious.

'You still want me to forbid them?' I asked.

'Yes, *meneer*.'

'Mr de Villiers,' I said, 'find out all you can about these boys. Then let me know.'

'And then,' I said to Spike, 'I'll talk to you about forbidding them.'

'They're a tough lot,' de Villiers told me later. 'No parental control. In fact they have left home and are living with George, the head of the gang. George's mother is quite without hope for her son, but she's old now and depends on him. He gives her money, and she sees nothing, hears nothing, says nothing. She cooks for them.'

'And they won't allow Spike to leave the gang?' I asked.

'I couldn't prove that, but it's a funny business. The reason why they don't want to let Spike go is because he has the brains and the courage. He makes the plans and they all obey him on the job. But off the job he's nobody. Off the job they all listen to George.'

'Did you see George?'

'I saw George,' he said, 'and I reckon he's a bad fellow. He's morose and sullen, and physically bigger than Spike.

'If you got in his way,' he added emphatically, 'he'd wipe you out – like that.'

We both sat there rather gloomy about Spike's future.

'Spike's the best of the lot,' he said. 'It's tragic that he ever got in with them. Now that he wants to get out . . . well . . .'

He left his sentence unfinished.

'Let's see him,' I said.

'We've seen these friends of Walter's,' I said to Spike, 'and we don't like them very much. But whether it will help to forbid their visits, I truly do not know. But I am willing to do what you say.'

'The Principal must forbid them,' he said at once.

So I forbade them. They listened to me in silence, neither humble nor insolent, nor affronted nor surprised; they put up no pleas or protests. George said, 'Good, sir,' and one by one they followed him out.

When a boy finally leaves the reformatory, he is usually elated, and does not hide his high spirits. He comes to the office for a final conversation, and goes off like one who has brought off an extraordinary coup. But Spike was subdued.

'Spike,' I said privately, with only de Villiers there, 'are you afraid?'

He looked down at the floor and said, 'I'm not afraid,' as though his fear were private also, and would neither be lessened nor made greater by confession.

He was duly married and de Villiers and I made him a present of a watch so that he could always be on time for his work. He had a good job in a factory in Industria, and worked magnificently; he saved money, and spent surprisingly little on clothes. But he had none of his old gaiety and attractive carelessness. He came home promptly, and once home, never stirred out.

It was summer when he was released, and with the approach of winter he asked if de Villiers would not see the manager of the factory, and arrange for him to leave half an hour earlier, so that he could reach his home before dark. But the manager said it was impossible, as Spike was on the kind of job that would come to a standstill if one man left earlier. De Villiers waited for him after work, and he could see that the boy was profoundly depressed.

'Have they said anything to you?' de Villiers asked him.

The boy would not answer for a long time, and at last he said with a finality that was meant to stop further discussion, 'They'll get me.' He was devoid of hope, and did not wish to talk about it, like a man who has a great pain and does not wish to discuss it, but prefers to suffer it alone and silent. This hopelessness had affected his wife and mother and sister, so that all of them sat darkly and heavily. And de Villiers noted that there were new bars on every door and window. So he left darkly and heavily too, and Spike went with him to the little gate.

And Spike asked him, 'Can I carry a knife?'

It was a hard question and the difficulty of it angered de Villiers, so that he said harshly, 'How can I say that you can carry a knife?'

'You,' said Spike, 'my mother, my sister, Elizabeth.' He looked at de Villiers.

'I obey you all,' he said, and went back into the house.

So still more darkly and heavily de Villiers went back to the reformatory, and sitting in my office, communicated his mood to me. We decided that he would visit Spike more often than he visited any other boy. This he did, and he even went to the length of calling frequently at the factory at five o'clock, and taking Spike home. He tried to cheer and encourage the boy, but the dark heavy mood could not be shifted.

One day Spike said to him, 'I tell you, sir, you all did your best for me.'

The next day he was stabbed to death just by the little gate.

In spite of my inside knowledge, Spike's death so shocked me that I could do no work. I sat in my office, hopeless and defeated. Then I sent for the boy Walter.

'I sent for you,' I said, 'to tell you that Spike is dead.' He had no answer to make. Nothing showed in his face to tell whether he cared whether Spike were alive or dead. He stood there impassively, obedient and respectful, ready to go or ready to stand there for ever.

'He's dead,' I said angrily. 'He was killed. Don't you care?'
'I care,' he said.

He would have cared very deeply, had I pressed him. He surveyed me unwinkingly, ready to comply with my slightest request. Between him and me there was an unbridgeable chasm; so far as I know there was nothing in the world, not one hurt or grievance or jest or sorrow, that could have stirred us both together.

Therefore I let him go.

De Villiers and I went to the funeral, and spoke words of sympathy to Spike's mother and wife and sister. But the words fell like dead things to the ground, for something deeper than sorrow was there. We were all of us, white and black, rich and poor, learned and untutored, bowed down by a knowledge that we lived in the shadow of a great danger, and were powerless against it. It was no place for a white person to pose in any mantle of power or authority; for this death gave the lie to both of them.

And this death would go on too, for nothing less than the reform of a society would bring it to an end. It was the menace of the socially frustrated, strangers to mercy, striking like adders for the dark reasons of ancient minds, at any who crossed their paths.

The Worst Thing of His Life

You never get used to absconding. I remember once we went for sixty-one days without an absconder; there were six hundred boys in the reformatory, and nearly half of them could have walked away at any time. Day after day went past of peace unbroken except for trifling offences, and you couldn't help being proud of it, though you kept your pride secret so that no hand out of the sky could strike you down for presumption. Then on the sixty-second day a boy ran away, and we were as downcast as though the sixty-one days had never happened. Somehow you never got used to it.

A time of heavy absconding was a trial of the soul. You felt as though the whole institution were cracking and breaking; you felt you were inefficient, a bungler, a theorist who had theories but no knowledge of human nature; you felt judged even by your own staff and your own boys.

And you feared too, although you didn't talk about it, that some newspaper would get hold of it, and print in some careless corner the words that would bring your career to an end, and kill the faith in your heart that your way was the right way, and make you nothing in the eyes of the world and your wife and children. For the Principal of a great institution has almost divine powers, and is admired by his friends and family.

Of course if your reformatory is what is called 'closed', then you can put the blame for absconding on to the perversity of human nature; you can join the public heartily when it curses your absconders. But when your reformatory is half 'open', and when you yourself made it so, you can't blame anyone but yourself. Of course if a staff member has been negligent, you can purge yourself by rebuking him beyond reason; but then you are ashamed, and you remember how he stood by you during some touble, so you go and apologise to him.

Half of your absconders are probably 'free' boys. Their absconding worries you more than the others, because they promised you certain things when you gave them their freedom. Some abscond and stay away; some abscond and after dark return secretly and sheepishly to your house; one got to Durban, four hundred miles away, and there gave himself up to the police.

If a 'free' absconder commits some serious offence while he is at large, that is hard to bear, because you feel directly responsible. It is sometimes difficult to decide whether to make a boy 'free', because although his conduct is exemplary, he perhaps committed some violent offence before he came to you. You are torn in two, because you wish by this encouragement to confirm him in his resolution to be law-abiding, yet you are afraid that he may endanger you and your career by some violent act.

When such a boy does abscond, and shortly afterwards some unknown person commits such an act, your mind is full of anxiety, and you fear the worst. You sleep badly at night, and dread the ringing of the telephone. Sometimes hundreds of police are called out after such an offence, and you are tormented by the thought that perhaps you are responsible for all this expenditure of time and effort, and for some innocent person's suffering.

After my first five years the reformatory began to settle down after having been disturbed by these new experiments. As far as absconding was concerned, the new freedom was working as well as the old strict watchfulness. But the new freedom liberated not only boys, but new energies and strengths from the unprofitable task of watching; one could now turn to the real work of education. Yet, though year succeeded year in comparative tranquillity, the old fear was never quite banished; the ring of the telephone, especially in the sleeping hours, was enough to set the heart beating.

One night after my wife and I had gone to bed, I was awakened by the sound of footsteps on the gravel outside the window, followed by a respectful knock.

'Who's there?' I asked.

'It's me, sir, Jonkers,' a voice said in Afrikaans.

If I could be called the colonel of the reformatory, then Jonkers was the adjutant, the chief executive officer. It was a tough job with a heavy responsibility, and a day that began at six in the morning and ended at six at night, with the likelihood of being called out at any time thereafter. He was a simple man of no great education, but with a loyalty and devotion that no man ever surpassed; he had stood by me in all kinds of crises and troubles, and in his simple way understood what I was doing and believed in it.

His voice was low and trembling, so I made mine matter-of-fact and firm and said, 'What's the matter?'

'There's great trouble,' he said.

He had never said that to me before, and I thought with pain, now it has come, just when we thought all danger was past.

'Go round to the front door,' I said.

I put on my dressing-gown and slippers, and said to my wife, 'It's some trouble.'

When I let Jonkers in, I was shocked by his appearance. The big man would not look at me, but with exaggerated politeness edged himself in at the door, and did not sit down till I had asked him to.

I sat down too, and said to him with fear in my heart, 'What's the trouble?'

He made no answer, but sat there trying to control himself and I sat watching him, both of us full of misery. But I put on a brave front to him, and waited quietly for him to speak, as though I had great resources on which to draw when the need would arise. Still he did not speak, and I said to him, 'Take your time.'

He said, with a kind of brave gratitude, *'Dankie, meneer.'* He sat there in front of me, humble and shaken, and did not know he was in fact tormenting me; he did not know he was in fact standing over me, with an axe or a club, and that I was crying out to him, 'For God's sake, strike me, but don't torment me.'

'You're upset,' I said.

Again he gave me the look of humble thanks. He was thanking me, the Principal with great powers, for noticing his suffering, as though it were kind of me, as though I were not sitting there consumed with desperate anxiety about myself and my work.

'I'm finished,' he said.

I did not know what he meant. He might have meant he was exhausted, all resources gone. Or he might have meant, and that would have been in character with him, that his career was finished. Because he would take the blame, I knew that. He would fear my wrath, but it would not occur to him that if he was finished, I would be finished too.

'It's the worst thing of my life,' he said.

'What is?'

'Sir, I can't bring myself to tell you,' he said. Then he said, 'I've told the Principal some bad news in my life, but I don't know how to tell him this.'

Then a car drew up outside the house, and doors banged, and men came running. And I thought, let them all come, and went out on to the stoep to meet them.

Fichardt said to me, 'Is Mr Jonkers here?'

'He's here,' I said.

'Thank God,' he said in a low voice. 'I was afraid he might do something desperate.'

And I said, also in a low voice, 'What's the trouble?' And I braced myself for the worst.

'It's his son, sir. He's just had a message to say his son's been arrested.'

So the great fear rolled off my heart, there on the stoep. The relief was so great that my whole self had to experience it, and for a moment, no, for some moments, I had no thought to spare for Jonkers and his son.

Then I said quietly, 'What for?'

'I don't know, sir.'

Fichardt and I went into the house, where Jonkers was sitting with his head in his hands.

'He's worried about the boy, sir,' said Fichardt. Then he added with meaning, 'He's worried about his job too.'

I went to Jonkers.

'Are you worried about the job?' I said.

He nodded and wept openly, a public servant in danger, and a father in disgrace.

'If they take away your job,' I said, 'they can take away mine too.'

The big man did not, could not, look at me, but I heard him saying in a broken voice, '*Dankie, meneer; dankie, meneer.*'

'I couldn't run this place without you,' I said.

Even in the midst of his weeping he could not hide his pride. Then he said to me, 'I'm ashamed. I'm an elder in the church. There's never been a thing like this in our family.'

I was full of confidence and strength.

'We'll go to the police,' I said. 'It's some boy's trick. Perhaps he was showing off in a car. I'll go and get dressed.'

Jonkers looked at me with gratitude. I could see that he was grateful to be going to the police with the Principal.

Fichardt went back to the car, and I went to get dressed.

'Trouble?' asked my wife.

'Trouble,' I said. 'But not the reformatory.'

'Good,' she said, and went to sleep.

When I got back to Jonkers, he was standing up waiting for me.

'*Meneer*,' he said.

'Yes.'

'I hope I didn't frighten you,' he said. 'You might have thought it was trouble at the reformatory.'

'Of course not,' I said, 'of course not.'

'I told my wife,' he said, 'I'm down as far as a man can go, but if I go to the Principal he'll lift me up.'

'That's good,' I said. 'Let's go.'

Sponono

This very day I received a letter from Sponono, full of reproaches. He asks why I have not answered his previous letter. He writes to me, 'Are you then like other people, who, when a man has done wrong, treat him badly? I have always looked upon you as trustworthy, but now I am ashamed in front of my friends.' He asks, 'Why have you turned? You were always a man of your word, but now you are changed.' He concludes that this turning of mine is 'wonderful'.

I feel I must put up some kind of defence against this indictment which questions qualities of my character of whose existence I have been moderately certain. Whether his friends will ever read it, and refrain from harsh judgments on that account, is very improbable. But it will at least give me the opportunity of describing an engaging rascal, who expected my conduct towards him to surpass in superhuman degree his conduct towards me. How did he ever formulate such noble ideals of behaviour? That I do not know, for he certainly did not practise them. Nevertheless he knew of them, and while he considered himself too frail to practise them, he expected me to do so, and never failed to reproach me when I fell short of them. Yet on one occasion he did practise them, under the most unlikely circumstances, with an ease and grace that would have done credit to a saint.

Sponono was a Xhosa boy, about sixteen years old when he first came to the reformatory. My first intimate encounter with him was certainly extraordinary. He had asked to see the Principal, on urgent private business, and accordingly he was brought to me by the Chief Supervisor, Mr van Dyk.

'Well, Sponono,' I said, 'I hear you want to see me.'

'Yes, *meneer*,' he said.

'What is your trouble?' I asked.

'I have no trouble,' he said. 'I have come to see you about the trouble of Johannes Mofoking.'

'Are you a friend of his?' I asked.

'I am not a friend of his,' he said, 'but I have heard about his case, and it is about his case that I wish to speak with you.'

By this time Mr van Dyk was looking somewhat uncomfortable, because it was a rule that any boy wishing to see me must first state his business clearly to the Chief Supervisor, unless he could claim that the matter was confidential and private. But I told Mr van Dyk to put himself at ease, and I said to Sponono, 'What about Johannes Mofoking?'

'We all know', he said, 'that Johannes Mofoking ran away from the reformatory, and that when he was captured and sent back here, he was in possession of a gold watch.'

'That is so,' I said.

'Some of us think,' said Sponono, 'that you are being too severe. Johannes admitted that he had stolen the watch, and he did not lie about it. This makes us think that he is not a bad fellow, and he himself does not wish to go to prison, but says he is willing to do some extra time in the reformatory to atone for what he has done.'

'That is very good of him,' I said.

'Sir,' said Mr van Dyk, 'I had no idea . . .'

'Do not trouble yourself,' I said. 'Sponono, you must know that I cannot conceal the theft of this watch from the police. Furthermore . . .'

'*Meneer*,' he said, 'we do not . . .'

'Excuse me, sir,' said Mr van Dyk. 'Sponono, you must not interrupt the Principal when he is speaking. It is not proper.'

'I ask pardon,' said Sponono, humbly. 'I did not mean to interrupt the Principal.'

'Go on,' I said.

'*Meneer*,' said Sponono, 'we do not ask you to conceal the theft of the watch from the police.'

'That is good of you,' I said.

'*Meneer*,' he said, ignoring my own interruption, 'we are satisfied that he should go to court. All we ask is that you should ask the court to send him back to the reformatory. Otherwise, he may grow into a bad fellow, and we are sure you do not wish this to happen.'

'He is getting old,' I said. 'He is nearly twenty.'

'I admit he is nearly twenty,' said Sponono. 'But he is not a bad fellow. But if he goes to prison, I fear he will become hard.'

'The reformatory is very full,' I said. 'We have more than six hundred boys now, and the reformatory is built for only four hundred.'

'My room is not full,' said Sponono. 'He can sleep there.'

'That is very good of you,' I said. It was the third time I had made such a remark, but of the sarcasm he took as little notice as before.

'I thought it would be wrong to send Johannes to prison,' he said. 'I told a lie to the Chief Supervisor when I said I had private business, because I knew that if I had told him my real business, he would not have allowed me to see you.'

'Do you not think it wrong to tell a lie?' I asked.

'Not to save a person,' he said.

'Mr van Dyk,' I said, 'bring Johannes to me.'

Johannes was brought, and I said to him, 'Johannes, I understand that you are ready to go to court, and to plead guilty to stealing this watch, but that you wish to be sent back to the reformatory.'

'That is true, *meneer*.'

'But,' I said, 'you are nearly twenty, and if you have not yet learned to stop stealing, what good will it do to teach you all over again?'

'I am learning,' he said, 'but not yet enough. If I come back here, I shall learn completely. But if I go to prison, I shall learn to steal more than before.'

'In that case,' I said, 'I shall ask the court to send you back here.'

'Thank you, *meneer*,' he said.

'Don't thank me,' I said. 'Thank Sponono. He was the one who spoke for you.'

Johannes turned to Sponono. 'Thank you,' he said.

'Do not thank me,' said Sponono. 'Thank the Principal. Without him I could have done nothing.'

It was about a month later that Sponono asked to see me again.

'Is it more private business?' I asked Mr van Dyk.

Mr van Dyk smiled at me in a reproachful manner.

'Sponono wishes to work in your garden,' he said.

'William is already working in my garden,' I said.

'Your garden is not properly cared for,' said Sponono. 'William is a good fellow, but he does not fully understand the work of a garden.'

'What must I say to William?' I asked. 'Must I say to him that you do not approve of his work in the garden, and that you have appointed yourself in his place?'

'I do not say that,' said Sponono. 'Let me work under him until he is discharged. That will be very soon.'

'How do you know that?' I asked.

'He told me,' he said.

'Did you arrange it between you?' I asked. And when he did not answer I asked again, 'Shall I tell William that he does not understand the work of a garden?'

'That would only make trouble,' he said. 'Let me work under him.'

I must report that Sponono did not prove a good subordinate. William would come and complain to me that Sponono would not do what he was told to do. Sponono would come and complain to me that William was inefficient, lazy, and dishonest. I was compelled to divide the garden into two portions, and I must admit that Sponono proved an excellent gardener. But between him and William there was endless friction, until William was discharged, and Sponono took command. Then Sponono began to complain about the new assistant, a very meek fellow named George. But things went reasonably smoothly until Christmas Day.

Christmas Day was a big day at the reformatory, with special meals, a sports meeting with prizes, and gifts of sweets for the younger and tobacco for the older boys. I returned home at sunset after a hot and tiring day, looking forward to our own family Christmas and pleasant relaxation. But I had hardly sat down with our guests when the telephone recalled me to the office, where a harassed Mr van Dyk introduced me to a distraught Mr Anderson, who told me the following disturbing tale.

Mr Anderson and his wife had packed a picnic basket that morning, and had found a shady spot on the eastern portion of the reformatory farm, where they had enjoyed a good lunch of Christmas fare and some iced beer, after which they had lain down in the grass for a pleasant siesta. But their siesta was to prove anything but pleasant. They had been wakened rudely by a boy in clothes identical with the reformatory uniform, a khaki shirt and khaki shorts. This boy had menaced them with a large stone, and had snatched up Mrs Anderson's hand-bag from the grass, and made off into the bushes. In the hand-bag was sixty pounds, in twelve five-pound notes, a whole month's earnings, and the distress of husband and wife was painful to see.

'I know I should have had permission,' said Mr Anderson, 'but there was no one to be seen, and it was an ideal spot for a picnic. At least, we thought it was until this terrible thing happened.'

'If it was one of our boys, Mr Anderson,' I said, 'I hope we shall be able to find him. Most of the boys were at the sports, and we naturally have to know precisely where each one is on such an occasion. Did you find everything correct, Mr van Dyk?'

'Everything correct, sir. The only boys not at the sports were the domestic servants. I think, sir, you should hear what Mr Wessels has to report.'

He brought in Mr Wessels, who reported that he had been on farm duty, and that while visiting the top portion of the farm, he had seen Sponono walking through the trees. Knowing that Sponono worked for me, he had contented himself with asking the boy where he was going, and Sponono had replied that I had given him leave to go walking on the farm. We showed Mr and Mrs Anderson several of the photographs of the domestic servants, Sponono's among them, but they were unable to identify the boy who had menaced them.

'Bring Sponono here please,' I said to Mr van Dyk. 'Mr and Mrs Anderson, and Mr Wessels, I'll ask you to retire to another office.'

'This is the stone that the boy carried,' said Mr van Dyk.

'Please leave it on the table,' I said.

When Sponono came in, his attention was immediately attracted by the stone, but thereafter he kept his eyes away from it, by an effort of will, I thought.

'Where did you go this afternoon, Sponono?' I asked.

'I went to the sports,' he said.

'Were you there all the time?' I asked.

'The Principal knows I don't like sports,' he said, 'so after a while I went for a walk.'

'Where did you walk?'

He closed his eyes for more perfect remembering.

'Down past the stables,' he said, 'then down to the fields, then back to the pump-house, then back to the house, *meneer*.'

'Did you see anybody?'

'No one, *meneer*.'

Then Mr Wessels came in, and Sponono looked at him warily.

'Mr Wessels saw you at the other end of the farm,' I said. 'He asked you where you were going, did he not?'

'That is true, *meneer*.'

'But you said you saw nobody.'

'Not by the stables,' he said. 'But I did see Mr Wessels at the top end of the farm.'

'Did you see anybody else?' I asked. 'Think carefully before you answer.'

'Nobody else,' he said.

'Why did you tell Mr Wessels I had given you leave to take a walk?' I asked.

'I did not quite say that,' he said. 'Probably Mr Wessels did not hear me clearly, as I do not speak his language very well. I told him I was looking for something for the Principal.'

'For what?' I asked sternly.

Against his will his eyes went back to the stone on the table.

'Stones,' he said.

'For what?' I asked.

'For your garden, *meneer*.'

'I did not ask you to get stones for the garden,' I said.

'I wanted them for a wall,' he said. 'I was going to speak to you tomorrow.'

I pointed to the stone on the table. 'Is that one of the stones you found?' I asked.

He did not answer. The questions were coming rapidly, and he was finding it difficult to judge which of the possible answers were the least dangerous. He was breathing heavily, and he found it impossible entirely to conceal his distress.

'Why do you not answer?' I asked.

'You are frightening me, *meneer*,' he protested.

'I am only asking you questions,' I said.

'I can see you are angry,' he said. 'Something bad has happened, and somebody wants to blame me for it.'

'What has happened?' I asked.

'Something bad.' He would say no more. The sweat was pouring off his face.

'Leave us, Mr Wessels,' I said. I sat down at my table, but I did not look at Sponono.

'The boy Johannes was saved from prison, because you told me I was doing wrong. Is that not so?'

'Yes, *meneer*.'

'Now it is your turn to be saved from wrong,' I said. 'You will not lie to me, will you?'

In a low voice, he said, 'No, *meneer*.'

'You went walking at the top end of the farm?'

'Yes, *meneer*.'

'You were contemplating nothing evil,' I said. 'You were thinking only of stones for my garden. You did not wish to hurt anybody.'

'No, *meneer*.'

'But,' I said, 'a great temptation was put in your way. And before you could gather your strength, you had done something wrong.'

He was silent, and if ever a silence gave consent, it was this one.

'But now,' I said, 'you repent of what you have done, and would like to make amends.'

In the low voice he said, 'Yes, *meneer*.'

I stood up. 'Let us go and get the money,' I said. 'It will be a great joy to these two people who thought they would have no Christmas at all.'

We went out and got into the car and he led me straight to the money, all sixty pounds of it. The Andersons were overjoyed, and Mr Anderson insisted on giving me ten pounds, and when I refused he wanted to give it to Mr Wessels, who naturally refused also. So he put it on my table, and I said I would send it to one of the Christmas funds.

'I feel almost', said Mr Anderson, so full was he with relief and gratitude, 'like giving something to the boy.'

'I understand your feelings,' I said drily, 'but I fear that the consequences of his act must be quite different.'

The consequences of Sponono's act were serious; he lost all his free privileges and was sent back to the security building, so that his term at the reformatory virtually began again. His offence was not reported to the police, because all reformatory offences except the gravest fell within my jurisdiction. Nevertheless he tried to get me to alter my decision.

'If I had run away and spent all this money,' he said, 'you would not have punished me more severely.'

When I admitted this, he said, 'What is more, *meneer*, I showed you where the money was hidden.'

'I am not a judge,' I said. 'My job is to teach you better ways, but I have not yet succeeded, therefore I must begin all over again.'

He could find no answer to this contention, so he said to me, 'I ask only one thing, *meneer*.'

'What is that?'

'I ask, *meneer*, that if I behave well, and if I again receive my freedom, I should be allowed to work again in your garden.'

'I am willing to agree to that,' I said.

'Is that a promise?' he asked.

I could see that Mr van Dyk was scandalised, but I smiled at him pacifyingly, and said to Sponono, 'It is a promise.'

He turned to Mr van Dyk and scandalised him further by saying, 'I am satisfied.'

Two weeks after that, Sponono had a fight with one of his fellows, and received a serious wound over the eye. The doctor told me that the sight of the eye was impaired, and what was more, that when the wound was healed, the eye itself would not look very pretty.

We investigated the case carefully, and came to the conclusion that both Sponono and his antagonist Tembo were equally blameworthy; but it was difficult to know how to deal with Tembo, for in a fight which had begun as a bout of fisticuffs, he had suddenly whipped off his heavy belt and struck directly at Sponono's face.

'What have you to say?' I asked Tembo. 'This is a grave offence that you have committed.'

'I know it is, *meneer*,' said Tembo. 'This is why I got permission to go to the hospital so that I could ask Sponono's forgiveness.'

'Did you forgive him?' I asked Sponono.

Sponono peered at me from under his bandages.

'I forgave him,' he said. 'He did not mean to hurt my eye. I might have hurt his eye too, if he had not hurt mine first. It was his bad luck, *meneer*.'

'You are a generous fellow,' I said to Sponono, 'and your forgiving spirit is an example to us. However, your forgiveness is between you and him; but between him and me is another matter.'

'You should find it easier to forgive him,' said Sponono, 'for it was my eye that was hurt, not yours.'

'You should have been a lawyer,' I said.

He smiled at me from beneath the bandages. '*Meneer*, you are playing with me. I am not clever enough to be a lawyer.'

'Listen, Sponono,' I said, 'you may forgive a person, and I may forgive him, but that does not mean that he should not bear the consequences of his act.'

His one eye looked at me sceptically, as though I were propounding a doctrine palpably false, but he was too polite to say so.

'Do you think,' I asked, 'that if a person is forgiven, his offence is wiped out as though it had never been done?'

'Yes,' he said.

'Tembo,' I said, 'you are dismissed with a reprimand. Your belt will be taken away from you, and a softer one will be given to you. If you will take my advice, you will not wear such a belt for the rest of your life, for your temper is hot, and will one day get you into serious trouble.'

Tembo said to me humbly, 'Thank you, *meneer*,' Mr van Dyk took him away, and I said to Sponono, 'Where did you get this idea of forgiveness?'

'It is the teaching of Jesus,' he said. He apparently had no idea of what I might be expected to know or not to know, for he added, 'Shall I get a Bible, so that I can read it to you?'

'No, you tell me,' I said.

'Jesus said that we must forgive those who offend against us, even unto seventy times seven.'

'Are you a Christian?' I asked.

'I am not,' he said. 'I am not good enough, but I like to obey the commandments.'

'Good luck to you,' I said. 'You may go.'

'Couldn't you forgive me now, *meneer*, instead of making me begin again from the beginning?'

'You committed a grave offence,' I said, 'for which I have forgiven you, but you must still begin again from the beginning.'

'Couldn't you forgive this much, *meneer*, that I could go now to work in your garden?'

'No,' I said. 'Not until you are free.'

He surveyed me out of his one eye, his learned superior who knew so little about the true meaning of forgiveness. What he saw was apparently discouraging, for he shrugged his shoulders.

'Why do you do that?' I asked.

'Because I see you are not ready,' he said.

I wished that Mr van Dyk could have been there, for he often thought I was ready to the point of foolishness. But I was denied that pleasure.

Two months later I took the decision to leave the service of the State, and therefore to leave the reformatory. I was obliged to give three months' notice and I tried to keep the news as secret as possible, but before long it was widely known. One of my first visitors was Sponono. His eye had healed better than expected, and had given him an incredibly knowing look; it remained half closed, as though he could have seen more of one's weaknesses had he opened it, but as though out of tolerance he would not do so, even though he would continue to give the impression that he knew all.

'I hear you are leaving, *meneer*.'

'That's true, Sponono.'

'You promised me', he said, 'that when I was free I could work in your garden.'

'That's true,' I said, 'but I did not know I would be leaving.'

'Where are you going to?' he asked.

'I am going to Natal,' I said.

'I have never been to Natal,' he said, 'but I am sure I could work very well there.'

I was going to say, 'That is very good of you,' when he suddenly changed his tactics, and addressed me gravely.

'I did not regard your promise as merely a promise that I could work in your garden,' he said. 'It was rather a promise that I could be near you, and that was very important to me, because then I knew I would not get into more trouble.'

'You did work near me,' I said, 'and you threatened two innocent people with a stone, and stole sixty pounds from them.'

He looked at me as though he were pained by the coarseness and directness of my language.

'You said you had forgiven me for that,' he said.

'I have forgiven you,' I said. 'But I thought I should remind you that being near me did not help you on that occasion.'

I could see that he thought that the reminder was unethical. But he did not pursue the argument.

'When I am discharged,' he said, 'I hope I may come to work for you.'

'The people in Natal are Zulus,' I said, 'and you might not be happy among them.'

'I shall be quite happy,' he said with finality. 'There are many Zulu boys here, and I have not fought with any of them.'

'When you are discharged,' I said, 'if I am still in Natal, and if I have a garden, you may come to work for me.'

Sponono turned to Mr van Dyk. 'I am satisfied,' he said.

I glanced at my Chief Supervisor, but he looked quite non-committal.

So that was how Spnono came to Natal. He had not been there long before he told me that Cele, the gardener, was an idle and worthless fellow, and that Jane Zondi, who looked after our house, was a loose and dishonest woman. These revelations I bore with fortitude, but his next escapade was beyond reason. He had been invited to a party at Jane's sister's home in the hills behind the coast, and, dissatisfied with the food, had killed one of the chickens and made himself a feast. He had also drunk freely, and made advances of an ugly and threatening nature to Jane's sister's daughter. The whole countryside was up in arms against the stranger, and Jane's sister went to the police. The police came to see me, saying that it was difficult to obtain evidence in such cases, but that they had no doubt that Sponono had broken several laws; however if I would send him back to the reformatory, they would take no further steps in the matter. Jane Zondi also came to see me and asked me to build an extra room for Sponono in another part of the garden, while Cele asked me to buy another garden and install Sponono there as sole and all-powerful gardener so that he could mismanage both the garden and his private affairs without involving others.

'No one seems to want you,' I said to Sponono.

'I can see that,' he said. 'From the time I came, they have all been against me; from the time they knew I came from the reformatory.'

'Who told them that?' I asked. 'It must have been you yourself.'

'Yes, I told them,' he said. 'I thought it would make them more patient with me.'

'The police say you have a choice,' I said, 'to go to court, or to go back to the reformatory.'

'These people hate me,' he said. 'It is better for me to go back.'

So Sponono went back to the reformatory, and so began my long correspondence with him, that has lasted now for ten years.

'Your action was very harsh,' he wrote. 'Others at the party behaved just as I did. You must not think I was the only one who ate the chicken. Jane's sister's son ate just as much as I did, and he was the one who informed against me.'

He also complained bitterly against Jane and Cele, and said that they were of the kind that would never forgive any person who had done wrong, but would hound him down until he was destroyed. Furthermore they were Zulus, and hated him because he was a Xhosa. Also Cele was afraid of him, because it was clear that Cele knew nothing about gardening, and was afraid of losing his job to a better person.

'But you,' he wrote, 'you ought to know better. You have worked with thousands of sinners, and have gained a good reputation amongst us. Also you are a white man, and have no reason to hate me. Lastly, you are a writer, not a gardener, and you could never lose your job to a person like myself.'

When Sponono had served a further year at the reformatory, it was decided to release him, and he asked to be released to me. However, I declined to take him. I wrote to him and told him that Jane Zondi was still with us, and Cele was still in the garden, and neither of them wished to have him.

'They are unforgiving,' he wrote, 'but that should not be your nature. Do not be influenced by them. Do not be afraid to take me. Why should I make trouble in my own father's house?'

I fear that my nature remained unforgiving. I wrote to him that he had failed me twice, and had twice caused trouble in my house. I asked him whether there was not perhaps some fault in his own character.

'I have many faults in my character,' he wrote, 'but we are speaking of you, not myself. It is true I have failed you twice, but that is a long way from seventy and seven.

'What can I do?' he asked. 'At one stroke you have taken away from me my home and my father.'

Now it so happened that I had a friend who was growing citrus in the Eastern Province. He was a tolerant fellow of the kind I had once supposed myself to be, and what is more, his employees were all Xhosas.

With him I got Sponono a job, which lasted for exactly six weeks, when he was found guilty of stealing a jacket and money from a fellow-employee, and was sent to the prison at East London for two years.

'A useless fellow,' my friend wrote to me. 'If you wanted to fire my enthusiasm for rehabilitation, why did you start off with such a quarrelsome scoundrel? He quarrelled with the other workers from the first day he landed here. His worst characteristic was that he was always reminding me of my paternal duties, which he claimed I had inherited from you. I should have thought that after your thirteen years at a reformatory, you would have known a bad egg when you saw one.'

'Your friend is a hard man,' wrote Sponono to me. 'He had all your sternness but none of your good-heartedness. After all, I offended only once against him.'

Sponono was allowed to write one letter a month, and I was his correspondent. I sent him simple books to read, and he discovered that the Superintendent of the prison had known me when I was in the State service.

'I admire your letters to Sponono,' the Superintendent wrote to me, 'but I'm afraid your admonitions are wasted. He is a bad-tempered prisoner, and I have had to give him some spells of solitary confinement for fighting. Nevertheless, go on with the good work.'

'The Superintendent is a hard man,' wrote Sponono. 'It is not like the reformatory here. There is no forgiveness for small offences.'

I do not know how this letter got past the eagle eye of the prison censor; in any event it was the last of its kind. For Sponono was due to be released, and again he asked if he could come back and work for me.

'Jane and Cele are still here,' I wrote, 'and they will not agree to your returning.'

'Who', he wrote and asked me, 'is the master in your house?'

It was some years before I heard from him again. This time he was in

Tiger Vlei, a prison for seven-year prisoners, who might however receive quite a generous remission for good behaviour. He was allowed to write only at rare intervals, and I replied to him, but I must admit it was with a waning enthusiasm. For one thing the new Government of South Africa had made it almost impossible for Africans from one part of the country to work in another. For another, I felt that my relationship with Sponono had reached its end.

'You take a long time to answer my letter,' he wrote. 'What is this change in you? There is no change in me.'

Nor did it look as though there ever could be. After five years he wrote that he was shortly to be released, and wanted to return to me. By that time I had moved to another part of the country. I was engaged in work that took me frequently away from home. I did not think of saddling my wife with the problem of Sponono.

'I cannot have you,' I wrote. 'I still have Zulus working for me, and you do not like them. I do not think it would be successful.'

It was then that he wrote to me that he had always looked upon me as trustworthy, but that now I made him ashamed among his friends.

'Why have you turned?' he asked. 'You were always a man of your word, but now you have changed.

'You do not say you cannot forgive me,' he wrote, 'but that is what you mean. But Jesus taught we must forgive unto seventy times seven.

'I do not quarrel any more,' he wrote. 'I have had a change of heart. So have you, but yours is in the wrong direction.'

Sponono, we have reached, you and I, what is called, in a game not known to you, a stalemate. You move, and I move, but neither of us will ever capture the other. I gave you your chance, and you would not take it, for reasons that are beyond either of us to explain. You gave me my chance, and I would not take it, for reasons that I thought sound and proper.

But I have no doubt that you wish, as I wish, that the game could have ended otherwise.

The Court

On top of the dais is the PRINCIPAL's *table and chair, and on the table is the Punishment Book. Upstage right is the Witness Box, and upstage left is the Prisoner's Dock.*

When the act begins, the drums play and the CHORUS *sings* NGEKE NGIYE KWAZULU. JOHANNES *opens the Warriors' Dance. When the* CHORUS *breaks into* INYANDA, SPONONO *and* ATTENDANT *enter from stage right.* SPONONO *is wearing a robe and a circlet. Underneath the robe he is still wearing his khaki shirt and khaki long trousers. He is greeted with great enthusiasm and cries of 'Sponono!' He begins to dance the twist with one of the girls from the* CHORUS. *Then imperiously he stops the singing and dancing. The* IMBONGI *calls out praises, which the* CROWD *approve. He ascends the dais and on his left stands his* CHIEF COUNCILLOR, *with a ceremonial stick.* SPONONO *raises his hand for silence. He sits.*

SPONONO
Bring him in.

(At one end of the grille appear the PRINCIPAL *and two more* WARRIORS. *We see that the* PRINCIPAL *is the prisoner. There is a buzz of excitement in the Court. The* WARRIORS *unlock the further gate, all go through, and the gate is locked. The nearest gate is unlocked; all go through, and the gate is locked. The* WARRIORS *escort the* PRINCIPAL *to the door, and stand, one on each side. The high grille is removed. The* PRINCIPAL *looks at the dock but does not enter it. He looks at* SPONONO. *He looks about him. It is obvious to him that this is a court.)*

PRINCIPAL
What is the charge?

SPONONO
(Gravely)

You are charged with desertion. You are charged with having deserted your duty. You are charged also with having deserted the teaching of your own religion. There cannot be a greater offence. But you can defend yourself. You can ask any questions. You can call any witness you like.

PRINCIPAL
I understand.

SPONONO
When a man is fighting for his life, he may kill. Even if he does not kill, he may inflict wounds.

PRINCIPAL
I understand.

SPONONO
What do you plead? Guilty or not guilty?

PRINCIPAL
I plead not guilty.

CHIEF COUNCILLOR
Bring Johannes Mofoking!
    (JOHANNES, *who has been taking part in the dance, goes to the Witness Box.*)

SPONONO
Johannes, you have not stolen again?

MOFOKING
No, *meneer*.

SPONONO
Your head, Johannes – does it still turn?

MOFOKING
No, *meneer*.

SPONONO

Why didn't you steal again, Johannes? Was it because you were forgiven?

MOFOKING

Yes, *meneer*.

SPONONO

Who forgave you?

MOFOKING

Sponono!
> *(There is a great wave of commendation in the Court.* IMBONGI *rises and calls out praises. There is a buzz of approval.* JOHANNES *leaves the Court, smiling.* SPONONO *raises his hand. All are silent.* IMBONGI *sits.)*

CHIEF COUNCILLOR

Call the small one!
> *(*CHORUS *sings the* LAMENT.
> HA'PENNY *enters very shyly from stage right.* ATTENDANT *leads him to the Witness Box. There is a murmur of excitement in the Court.* SPONONO*'s face lights up with pleasure at the sight of the small boy.* HA'PENNY *goes into the box, but he cannot be seen. A stool is brought for him to stand on. The* CHORUS *stops.* SPONONO *comes down to the Witness Box.)*

SPONONO

What's your name?

HA'PENNY

(Just audible. His speech is always just audible.)
Ha'penny, *meneer*.

SPONONO

What's your other name?
> *(No reply)*

Have you any family?
> *(No reply)*

Didn't you have Mrs Maarman? And Richard and Dickie and Anna and Mina?
    (No reply)
In your thoughts?

                    HA'PENNY
    (He smiles.)
Yes, *meneer*.

                    SPONONO
And you played with them in your thoughts?

                    HA'PENNY
Yes, *meneer*.

                    SPONONO
And you got letters in your thoughts?

                    HA'PENNY
Yes, *meneer*.

                    SPONONO
    (His voice shakes the Court.)
And this man said to you, 'Show me one of the letters that you get in your thoughts.'

                    HA'PENNY
    (Nodding, but not audible. The question, and the loudness of SPONONO's voice, have frightened him.)
Yes.

                    SPONONO
And you could not?

                    HA'PENNY
Yes.

                    SPONONO
And you were afraid that if you couldn't, your thoughts would die?

HA'PENNY
Yes.

SPONONO
(Moderating his voice a little)
And you were afraid . . . that if your thoughts died . . . then perhaps . . . you . . .

PRINCIPAL
(Leaving the dock and thundering)
In God's name, what are you trying to do? Must the child go through all this again? Didn't you call yourself the Protector of the Small Ones? Must he go through this agony again?

SPONONO
(Swiftly and angrily)
Who made the agony?

PRINCIPAL
I did it to save him from a worse one. I didn't want him to go back there and be rejected. So I decided to break his fantasy.

SPONONO
And you broke his heart as well.

PRINCIPAL
I wanted him to face reality.

SPONONO
Keep your big words. We're talking about deeds here.

PRINCIPAL
If you want to talk about deeds, call the two visitors.

SPONONO
(In anger, and without thought)
All right, call them.

CHIEF COUNCILLOR
(Rising)
Bring the two visitors!

SPONONO
Ha'penny, you can go now. But wait for me outside.
>   *(HA'PENNY leaves box and crosses to stage centre where he is surrounded by CHORUS and others, who call out many things to him. SPONONO returns to the Bench. He sits. HA'PENNY goes off stage left. By this time, MR and MRS MAKATINI are in the box. They are awed by the Court as they were by the reformatory.)*

PRINCIPAL
(Now standing before the Witness Box)
Mrs Makatini, you remember Christmas Eve in the Visitors' Room?

MRS MAKATINI
I'll never forget it, *meneer*.

PRINCIPAL
You remember the first boy, the nice one, who said he would find your son Henry?

MRS MAKATINI
Yes, I remember him.

PRINCIPAL
And you remember the second boy, the one who knocked you both over and took your money?

MRS MAKATINI
Yes.

PRINCIPAL
Do you remember him, Mr Makatini?

MR MAKATINI
Meneer – well, you see –
>   *(He laughs his loud, inappropriate laugh.)*

I was not remembering very well.
>   (*As once before, he looks as though he has made a fool of himself.*)

PRINCIPAL

But do you remember that the first boy and the second boy were proved to be the same?

MR MAKATINI

Yes, I remember that.

PRINCIPAL

Do you remember his name?

MRS MAKATINI

His name was Sponono!
>   (*The* IMBONGI *has been drowsing, but he gets his cue, and he stands up and begins his praises. He ceases when he sees the disapproving looks of all.* SPONONO *looks down.*)

PRINCIPAL

Mrs Makatini, when he took your money, did you cry out?

MRS MAKATINI

Yes. I cried out, 'Please don't take our money! That's our Christmas, for ourselves and our family!'

PRINCIPAL

And when he heard you cry, did he show mercy?

MR MAKATINI

No, *meneer*. He said, 'To hell with your Christmas.'
>   (PRINCIPAL *half-bows to* SPONONO *and returns to the dock.*)

SPONONO

>   (*Standing*)

But in spite of all this, you were willing to forgive him?

MRS MAKATINI

Yes.

SPONONO
Then why was he not forgiven?

MRS MAKATINI
The Principal would not forgive him.

SPONONO
(*To* MR MAKATINI)
What did the Principal say?

MR MAKATINI
Judge . . . well, you see . . .
(*He laughs his nervous laugh.*)
I was not remembering well.

MRS MAKATINI
(*Thinking hard*)
Something . . .
(*She gets it*).
Something about the . . . con . . . quince . . . conquincences.

SPONONO
That the boy must bear the consequences of his act?

MRS MAKATINI
Yes. Yes, that was it.

SPONONO
Why did you want to forgive him?
(*But she does not know.*)
Was it not, Mrs Makatini, because you hoped that if you forgave him, that the second boy would grow more and more like the first one, until the only one was the good one after all?

MRS MAKATINI
(*With admiration*)
Yes, that is what I thought.

SPONONO

You're a wise woman, Mrs Makatini.
    (MRS MAKATINI *is delighted.*)

MRS MAKATINI
    (*Earnestly*)
Judge . . . Judge, what became of the second boy?

SPONONO

What became of the . . .
    (*The question is for* SPONONO *quite devastating.*)

CHIEF COUNCILLOR
    (*Quietly to the two visitors*)
You may go.
    (MRS MAKATINI *smiles and bows to* SPONONO *but he does not see her. They go.*)
Bring Spike Moletsane.
    (SPIKE *saunters in from stage right as gaily dressed as ever. He takes his place confidently in the box.* SPONONO *recovers as he sees* SPIKE, *and he looks at him with affection.*)

SPONONO
    (*Intimately as he comes down from the dais*)
How are you, Spike?

SPIKE

Well, *meneer.*

SPONONO
    (*Coming down to the box*)
What did they do to you, Spike?

SPIKE

Oh! They paid me out.

SPONONO

For being reformed?
    (*They both laugh at the joke.*)

The trouble was, you had the brains. While you were there with the lanie, everything went wrong with them. They were waiting for just one thing, and that was for you to come back again.
(He laughs.)
And then you tell them you're reformed! *God*, were they angry!
(He grows serious, and looks at the PRINCIPAL.*)*
Why didn't you carry a knife?

SPIKE
The lanie said no. He told me I could carry a stick.

SPONONO
A stick! Did he think you were getting old?
(They laugh. Then SPONONO *grows serious.)*

SPONONO
How many were there?

SPIKE
There were five.

SPONONO
Who were they?

SPIKE
I couldn't see.

SPONONO
(Taking off his cap)
Was I one?

SPIKE
(Looking closely at SPONONO *and then laughing with joy. He comes out of the box.)*
Sponono! Sponono!
(In his joy SPIKE *goes to embrace* SPONONO, *but* SPONONO *holds him off.)*

SPONONO
Was I one?

SPIKE
Never! Never! You were my friend.
>*(They then embrace each other, hold each other's hands and smile at each other with joy.)*

SPONONO
>*(Looking at* SPIKE*'s shoes)*

Still smart, eh?

SPIKE
>*(Laughing)*

And you? You're a big man now. We always said you were too clever for that school. Too clever for the lanie too.
>*(They laugh.* CHORUS *and* SPIKE*'s old friends crowd round, greeting him.*
>*They all sing* FOR HE'S A JOLLY GOOD FELLOW.*)*

SPONONO
>*(He makes* SPIKE *sit, and sits himself. With a gesture that means he is talking about heaven)*

Tell me, Spike, how is it there?

SPIKE
It's O.K.
>*(They laugh.)*

But it's quiet. Too quiet!
>*(They laugh.)*

We sing a lot . . . but the songs . . .
>*(His face indicates that he does not think too much of the songs.)*

. . . you know!
>*(They laugh.)*

Sometimes I wish I was back in Victoriatown.
>*(They laugh.)*

Tell me, how is Elizabeth?
>*(The laughter stops dead.* SPONONO *retreats from* SPIKE.*)*

SPONONO
>*(Thundering, but still keeping his back turned)*

You are not here to ask questions, but to answer them.

(All SPIKE's *gaiety is gone. Humiliated, he comes down the steps. He turns once again to* SPONONO.*)*
You have shamed this Court. You may go.
*(*SPIKE *descends, not knowing what to do.)*

SPONONO

(Thundering)
Leave the Court!
(Two WARRIORS *come, and* SPIKE *leaves the Court between them.* CHORUS *sings,* COME WALK WITH ME. *In his rage,* SPONONO *comes down from the dais.)*
You call yourself a Christian?

PRINCIPAL

Yes.

SPONONO

Did you ever think that a man might do wrong, and that there might be only one consequence of his act, and that was to be forgiven?

PRINCIPAL

Yes.

SPONONO

Even to seventy times seven?

PRINCIPAL

Yes.

SPONONO

But you couldn't forgive like that. You said you forgave me but I must bear the consequences of my act.

PRINCIPAL

I did. It was the only kind of forgiveness for you. Without consequences, you would have promised anything. You would have promised . . .

SPONONO

(With anger and fear)

Silence!

(He speaks theatrically to the Court.)

That's the kind of man he was. He was supposed to be the father of us all. But if we asked for bread, he'd give us a stone.

(A brilliant idea occurs to him.)

If we asked for a knife, he'd give us a stick.

(He continues as before.)

If we asked him for fish, he'd give us a scorpion.

PRINCIPAL

(With asperity)

It was a serpent, not a scorpion.

SPONONO

You see, he knows the words. It was the meanings he didn't know. He believed we must bear the consequences of our acts. He wanted an eye for an eye, and a tooth for a tooth.

PRINCIPAL

I did not.

SPONONO

You did. Call Walter.

(He goes back to the dais. The IMBONGI calls his praise. When he is seated, he signs for the praises to end.)

CHIEF COUNCILLOR

Call Walter Masinga!

(He sits. WALTER enters. He takes his place in the Witness Box. He looks round the Court with concealed contempt. He does not even take off his cap. He is chewing gum.)

SPONONO

(He behaves ambivalently towards WALTER. He hates him, but still more does he wish to humiliate the PRINCIPAL.)

When you were at the school, you fought with another boy, and you struck him in the eye with your belt?

WALTER

Yes.

SPONONO

Were you punished?

WALTER

No.

SPONONO

(*Angrily*)
When you speak to me, you will say, 'Yes, *meneer*, No, *meneer*.' Do you understand?

WALTER

Yes . . . *meneer*.

SPONONO

And for God's sake, take that gum out of your mouth.
(*Pause*)
Were you completely forgiven, with no punishment, no consequences?

WALTER

Yes, *meneer*.

SPONONO

Was your life changed by this forgiveness?

WALTER

(*Coolly calculating*)
Yes, *meneer*.

SPONONO

You never used your belt again?

WALTER

No, *meneer*.
(*With veiled insolence*)
You see, I was changed, *meneer*.

SPONONO
Who forgave you?

WALTER
It was Sponono.
> (*There is a wave of commendation. The* IMBONGI *shouts praises.* WALTER *looks on inscrutably.* SPONONO *looks at the* PRINCIPAL. *He holds up his hand for silence. All sit.*)

SPONONO
Who killed Spike Moletsane?

WALTER
> (*On his guard*)

I don't know, *meneer*.

SPONONO
You know that five of them killed him?

WALTER
Yes, *meneer*.

SPONONO
Do you think Sponono was one?

WALTER
No, *meneer*.

PRINCIPAL
What are you trying to do? Are you trying to find out who killed Spike? Or is the only purpose . . .
> (*He gestures.*)

. . . of all this . . . to humble me?

SPONONO
You also killed him. You would not let him carry a knife.

PRINCIPAL
All right. I might have killed him. And so might you. Don't you

think he might have killed him too?
> (*The* CHIEF COUNCILLOR *has risen and is standing behind* SPONONO. *He whispers something to him. All the players gather round* SPONONO. SPONONO *is pleased with what he hears. He nods vigorously. All the company cries out,* 'YES!' *They return to their places.* IMBONGI *brings a stand to upstage centre.* CHIEF COUNCILLOR *comes down to* PRINCIPAL. *While he is coming down, a* COURT ATTENDANT *brings a pot of boiling water and places it on the stand.*)

CHIEF COUNCILLOR
> (*Who has come down to the dock*)

Do you know the ordeal of the water?
> (*A diviner, or* ISANGOMA, *in appropriate dress comes into the Court from the stage right.*)

Is everything ready?

ISANGOMA
Everything is ready.
> (*Offstage right there is great excitement, the beating of drums, the ululation of women. The* ISANGOMA'S ATTENDANTS *enter, carrying the pot of boiling water. They place it between the dock and the Witness Box. There is singing and dancing. Then the* ISANGOMA *calls for silence. The* CHIEF COUNCILLOR *comes down and goes to the* PRINCIPAL.)

PRINCIPAL
> (*Looking at* SPONONO)

Yes, I know it.

CHIEF COUNCILLOR
You will put your hand into the boiling pot, and bring out the pebbles for me. If you are innocent, you will come to no harm. If you are guilty . . .
> (*He calls.*)

Isangoma!
> (*Drums usher in* ISANGOMA. ISANGOMA *starts dancing and singing* ABAGULAYO. *Company forms a semi-circle with* ISANGOMA *at centre. They are kneeling and clapping as she sings. She goes through*

the preliminaries of smelling out. They all show fear.)

ISANGOMA

Who is the first?
(All look to SPONONO *for his decision. Dramatically he stands.)*

SPONONO

I am the first.
(He comes down and stands by the dock. He speaks to the PRINCIPAL.*)*
Now you will see.
(He goes to stand by the boiling pot, and the INSANGOMA *dances around him. He stands proudly. When she is finished, he bares his right arm. He gives a last look at the* PRINCIPAL. *He puts his right arm into the pot. He keeps it there longer than he need. He brings out the pebbles and gives them to the* CHIEF COUNCILLOR *who receives them deferentially.* SPONONO *shows his arm which is unscathed. His performance is greeted by great excitement. The* IMBONGI *calls out new praises.* SPONONO *goes to the dock and talks to the* PRINCIPAL. *Pulling down his sleeve)*
Do you believe it now?
Would you like to be excused? Shall I tell the Court you have asked to be excused?

PRINCIPAL

(Curtly)
No.
(He leaves the dock and goes to the ordeal. ISANGOMA *dances around him. When she is finished, he puts his arm into the pot. The* PRINCIPAL *keeps his arm there almost as long as* SPONONO *kept his. Then he brings out the pebbles and gives them to the* CHIEF COUNCILLOR. *The* IMBONGI *begins to praise the* PRINCIPAL. CROWD *cheers.* SPONONO *silences them. The* PRINCIPAL *examines his arm critically, almost as though he finds the result rather surprising. He makes a little gesture which might say, 'Well, what do you think of that?' He pulls down his sleeve and goes back to the dock, giving* SPONONO *a quizzical glance as he passes.* SPONONO *cannot conceal his displeasure. He climbs back to the Bench.* WALTER *clings fast to the railings of the Witness Box. He has watched the ordeals with dread.)*

CHIEF COUNCILLOR
Walter Masinga!

>(ISANGOMA *goes to the dock, and by dancing and gestures lures* WALTER *to the ordeal. He is terrified, but she more or less hypnotises him. He goes to the pot and she performs her dance. When she is finished he lifts the lid of the pot. Suddenly he hurls it down and breaks away to stage right. But as he tries to break through the semi-circle, he is caught by two of the* WARRIORS. WALTER *digs in his heels, but they drag him back to the pot, while he shouts out prayers and curses. At the pot the* WARRIORS *relax, and* WALTER *breaks again, and runs up the steps to the Judge's Seat. The crowd falls silent.)*

WALTER
Save me, *meneer!* Save me!

>*(He throws himself down before the Bench and* SPONONO *stands up.)*

SPONONO
(With aversion)
Don't touch me!
So you killed him?

WALTER
It was George, *meneer!*

SPONONO
It was five of you.
>*(No reply)*

So you went out that night to Victoriatown?

WALTER
Yes, *meneer.* It was George . . .

SPONONO
Silence! So you used the secret door?

WALTER
Yes, *meneer.*

SPONONO

And five of you, five of you, waited for him. Five of you killed the best friend of all my time. Five of you put your knives into his back.
    (He is overcome by emotion, and by his memory of SPIKE.*)*
Have you anything to say before I sentence you?

WALTER

    (Abjectly taking off his cap)
Yes, *meneer*. It was George, *meneer*. He made me go. He told me if I did not go, they would get me too.
    (He tries to come nearer to SPONONO, *because the* WARRIORS *are coming nearer to him. They seize him.)*
Don't let them take me, *meneer*! Please don't let them take me! Save me, *meneer*!
    (They take WALTER *down, but he breaks away again, and climbs the steps.)*

SPONONO

    (With extreme aversion)
Don't touch me.
    *(*WALTER *has been studying* SPONONO's *face for a sign. He ceases whining and adopts a pious tone.)*

WALTER

Can't you forgive me, *meneer*? Like you forgave me before, *meneer*?

SPONONO

The time you changed so deeply?

WALTER

Yes, *meneer*.

SPONONO

    (He is considering deeply. His emotions are again in conflict: hatred of WALTER *and the desire to humiliate the* PRINCIPAL. *He looks directly at the* PRINCIPAL. *He takes up the Punishment Book. He speaks to* WALTER.*)*
You have committed a grave offence. I ask myself, should you not be punished? I ask myself, should you not bear the consequences of

your act? Then I hear you ask me to be forgiven. And I say to you, you are forgiven.
(*He puts down the book.*)
For God's sake, take him away.
(*The* WARRIORS *take* WALTER *away. The* ISANGOMA *and* ATTENDANTS *remove themselves and their paraphernalia. The* CHIEF COUNCILLOR *returns to his seat.* SPONONO *is still standing. He speaks to the* PRINCIPAL.)
Have you any more defence?
(PRINCIPAL *struggles with himself.*)
Don't be afraid. I'm asking you.

PRINCIPAL
You said I could inflict wounds?

SPONONO
Yes.

PRINCIPAL
(*At last*)
Then call Elizabeth.

SPONONO
(*He also struggles with himself. Then he seems to decide that it is better to finish the matter once and for all.*)
Call her.

CHIEF COUNCILLOR
(*Rises*)
I call Elizabeth.

(*He sits.*
ELIZABETH *enters the Court. She is dressed in her bridal dress. She looks what she is, tender and beautiful. The* ATTENDANT *guides her to the Witness Box. The* PRINCIPAL *has left the dock and has come forward to question her. Then she recognises* SPONONO, *and she retreats towards the* PRINCIPAL. *The* PRINCIPAL *gestures, showing her she must go into the box.*
She goes into the box.)

PRINCIPAL
(At the box)
Elizabeth!

ELIZABETH
Yes, *meneer*.

PRINCIPAL
Did you love Spike, Elizabeth?

ELIZABETH
Yes, I loved him, *meneer*. He would have been a good husband to me . . . but the time was too short.

PRINCIPAL
When he asked you to marry him, did he promise you to obey the law?

ELIZABETH
Yes.

PRINCIPAL
Did he later ask you if he could carry a knife?

ELIZABETH
Yes.

PRINCIPAL
What did you say?

ELIZABETH
I told him no.

PRINCIPAL
You knew what might happen?

ELIZABETH
Yes.

PRINCIPAL
And if he could come again, and ask you again, what would you tell him?

ELIZABETH
I would tell him no. Ah! It wasn't easy, *meneer*. Like being caught between two ways, and both ways dangerous. That happens to us, *meneer*.

PRINCIPAL
Both ways were dangerous, Elizabeth. So how did you choose?

ELIZABETH
Well . . . I just chose, *meneer*. You see, *meneer*, I wanted our children to have a father who was good. I wanted them to have a father like . . .
    (Shyly)
like you, *meneer* . . . I wanted him to be honest at his work . . . I wanted him to think of his children first . . . so that they could feel safe . . . I wanted to feel safe too . . . Was that wrong, *meneer*?
    (The PRINCIPAL shakes his head. She continues confidentially.)
I would have been safe with Spike. If he promised to do something, I knew it would be done. And not all the boys in Victoriatown were like that. Some of them . . .

SPONONO
    (Thundering)
Silence!
    (He leaves the dais. She leaves the Witness Box and goes to stand near the dock.)
So you wanted a husband who was good, and all you got was one who was dead.
Let the Court be cleared.
    (All turn their backs on SPONONO and the PRINCIPAL. SPONONO is no longer arrogant. He drops his robe and circlet on the floor. He stands before the PRINCIPAL. He is on a slightly lower level than the PRINCIPAL.)

What shall I do now, *meneer*?
   (No answer)
Shall I marry her?
   (No answer)
You heard what she said. Her children must have a father who is good.
   (No answer)
I can be good, *meneer*. I can make her a promise.
   (No answer)
Speak, *meneer*.
   (There is still no answer and he speaks angrily.)
How can you say such a thing! Don't you know if you say such a thing, you can make it come true? Why are you so hard? Why have you always been so hard on me? Jesus taught we must forgive to seventy times seven, but how many times did you forgive me?
   (His grief is real.)
You always wanted a reward for your forgiveness. You would forgive me only if I didn't sin any more.
   (Angrily)
Who is as good as that? Are you as good as that?
   (No reply)
Have you no defence?

PRINCIPAL

You heard what Elizabeth said, that it happens to us, two ways and both dangerous, and we choose the one we think is best. So it was always between you and me.

SPONONO

There was only one man in the world who had any power over me
   (His voice rises in despair.)
. . . only one man who could have said to me, 'Don't believe it, it isn't true, no man is beyond saving, no man is utterly bad, no man can sin a sin that cannot be forgiven.'
   (He puts his hands on the edge of the dock, and he puts his head on his hands. The PRINCIPAL *comes to the edge of the dock and puts his hand on* SPONONO's *head. They stay like that for a while. Then* SPONONO, *his face contorted with anger and grief, breaks away.)*
Are you guilty or not guilty?

PRINCIPAL
I am guilty!
> (SPONONO *climbs back to his Bench. He claps his hands. The* IMBONGI *begins praises, but* SPONONO *silences him, and the Court reassembles. He sits. They all sit.*)

SPONONO
This case is ended. Before you all, I ask the prisoner: Are you guilty or . . .

MR MABASO
> (*Although the* WARRIORS *have tried to restrain him, he has forced his way into the Court and he interrupts* SPONONO.)

Who are you to find him guilty? Who made you a judge? Who are you to make us weep because your father struck your mother down, and lifted her up and struck her down again?
> (SPONONO *looks at him angrily.*)

You said your father left your mother with no hope. That wasn't true. You were her hope. Who promised her all the things she hadn't had? Who promised her, and failed her, and was forgiven, and promised her again? She could forgive till seventy times seven, and what good did it do?
> (SPONONO *hides his face. He cannot look at* MABASO *any more.*)

And then came the day when you struck her down . . .

PRINCIPAL
> (*He leaves the dock and goes to* MABASO.)

For God's sake, stop it, Mabaso! Don't you know we're beyond all that?
> (MABASO *looks at the* PRINCIPAL. *He gives a despairing shrug of his shoulders and leaves the Court. All look at* SPONONO *anxiously. The* PRINCIPAL *speaks to him.*)

I'm ready!
> (*The grille is placed in position.*)

SPONONO
Before you all, I ask the prisoner: Are you guilty or not guilty?

                    PRINCIPAL
I am guilty.

                    SPONONO
Do you ask for forgiveness?

                    PRINCIPAL
    (Gravely)
I do.

                    SPONONO
How can you be forgiven? You deserted your duty. Oh, you were wonderful. You gave us many things. But yourself you never gave . . .
    (To the WARRIORS)
Take him from here, and put the mark of Cain on his brow, and let him wander on the face of the earth, because he did not know he was his brother's keeper.
    (CHORUS sings with drums CRESCENDO, then SOFT MELODY, then INYANDA, which persists to the end. The reformatory bell starts ringing.
    All stand except SPONONO. The PRINCIPAL comes out of the dock and goes off between the two WARRIORS. The first gate is opened. The first gate is closed. SPONONO stands. The reformatory bell rings louder and louder and faster and faster and faster. SPONONO comes down from the dais and stands at the first gate. PRINCIPAL turns and sees him standing there.
    PRINCIPAL takes a step toward SPONONO but SPONONO makes a slight movement of retreat. PRINCIPAL turns and goes towards the second gate.
    FIRST WARRIOR opens gate and goes through. PRINCIPAL and SECOND WARRIOR go through. FIRST WARRIOR begins to lock the gate.
    SPONONO seizes bars of front gate.)
Meneer, meneer, I did not mean it!
    (PRINCIPAL turns again.)
I did not mean it, *meneer*!
    (FIRST WARRIOR completes locking of the second gate.)
Meneer, come back, *meneer*!

(CHORUS stops singing.
SPONONO *falls on his knees at first gate.* PRINCIPAL *comes closer to second gate and stretches out his hand.* SPONONO *stretches out his hands, while the bell rings softly.)*

CURTAIN

APPENDIX: BACKGROUND READING

SOME THOUGHTS ON EDUCATION AND REFORM

(Addresses given at the National Social Welfare Conference, 1944, and the Penal Reform League of South Africa National Conference, 1949.)

1. THE MORAL COMMUNITY

Quite apart from psychological and psychiatrical treatment, there is one very simple method of treatment which in South Africa is not applied at all but which should be applied to all amenable offenders. This is quite simply to make a community of the offenders, to increase with passage of time the freedom they enjoy, the responsibilities they shoulder, the privileges they earn, the temptations they encounter, till they are ready to return to society under the supervision of officers attached to the staff of the institution. This is moral education, and it is what they will need most. And alongside of it will be such vocational and other education as in process of time will be found valuable.

I cannot stress enough the importance of this moral education. Inside the institution one says nothing to the offender of the shortcomings of society; one is concerned only with his shortcomings. He is made to feel – however confused may be our own minds – that he is responsible for his actions, and that temptation must be resisted by the good man. His upward progress is made visible by the according of privileges and responsibilities; for the first time maybe in his life he undergoes the remedial experience of public recognition and approval. Privileges and responsibilities are given in public, and he affirms publicly his receipt of them and his determination to deserve them. Offenders, wise though they may be in the ways of the world, are children in their desire to win approval, and who knows but that here one has stumbled upon the deepest hunger of all mankind – to count for something in the eyes of one's neighbours. It should be clear that, however moving this picture of a programme may be, the programme is based on scientific and not sentimental considerations. The prison for amenable offenders would be strict, not soft and directionless. Rebuke would be stern, disgrace not unknown. But once accorded, they would be done with, and the patient work of rebuilding and re-education would be immediately renewed.

2. DEALING WITH DELINQUENCY

I for some years had the extraordinary experience, almost unknown to Public Servants, of administering the Diepkloof Reformatory under no regulations at all, and this meant a freedom to experiment such as comes to few of us in our lifetimes. And when the regulations came, they were based on the practices of the institutions, and have never restricted and confined them.

The foundation of these regulations, and indeed of the Children's Act itself, was the recognition of the profound truth that a law-breaking child is a child, that he has closer affinities to the child than to the law-breaker, and that as a child he has to be helped and protected, not judged and punished. This recognition was long delayed, partly due to the theories of heredity, which regarded the child as uneducable, and to our ultra-moralistic attitude to the whole question of free-will and choice. But the growing volume of evidence that laid such heavy responsibility on environmental influences could no longer be denied. And with this growing scientific understanding came also a realisation of the grave responsibility and duty of society towards its delinquent children, and that they were being expected to resist forces that a child least of all can resist.

I should like to set out briefly the guiding principles that should guide every civilised society in its dealings with delinquent children:

(1) At all costs the delinquency should be detected early. For delinquency roots itself, and if it is associated with profound inadequacies and inferiorities and insecurities, and if it roots itself in a child who is being denied the deep needs of his own nature, it may well prove ineradicable.

(2) If at all possible, the child must be taught to adjust in the very environment where he is failing.

(3) If removal of the child is necessary, it should be to an environment as like that of the home as can be achieved, e.g. to foster-parents or to a hostel-home.

(4) Only if this fails, or if it is from the outset impracticable, should he be removed to the industrial school or reformatory.

(5) If he is to be removed at all, attention should be turned, during his absence, to the home in which, and perhaps because of which, his delinquency developed.

3. THE REMEDIAL COMMUNITY

Education is not solely a matter of the impact of personality on personality; it is just as importantly a matter of the impact of environment on personality, and it is the task of an institution to create a remedial community, by the mere participation in whose life the child is strengthened in habits of industry, obedience, reliability, punctuality and trustworthiness. Indeed it is very wrong to suppose that education is solely a matter of instruction, teaching, preaching, admonition and correction. There may be times when this is necessary, but the greatest tasks of education must be carried out by a non-instructing, non-teaching, non-preaching, non-admonishing community, in which a child is led on from stage to stage to participate in a mode of living in which the great silent forces of example, and of laws and customs unconsciously adopted and obeyed, are the greatest operating factors. The child may well have reached a stage when he is unable to profit any further from personal and intimate attention, from instruction and admonition, unless these things are actively and plainly related to the life of the community in which he shares.

We need therefore not be concerned about the dangers of institutionalisation, if that institution is a purposeful and meaningful community, in which the child passes from stage to stage, each advance bringing with it greater privileges, greater responsibility, and greater physical freedom. He is living and learning, and as he advances the institutional supports are removed from him one by one, so that when he is ready to leave he has acquired some self-trust, some self-reliance, some self-respect.

You must not understand me to say that personal and intimate attention is unnecessary, that psychiatric and psychological services have no value, that an institution must not be comprised of a number of smaller groups which compensate for the defects of mass education. But this I must point out, that in my long experience the child who needs the most individual attention is often the least likely ever to be cured. Some children go out of their way to attract individual attention. We had a boy at Diepkloof who, whenever he was made free, broke into staff-houses. The whole behaviour was so purposeless that one suspected at once that the real purpose was not the apparent purpose, that he suffered from deep disturbances that the ordinary educator could not understand. It is in such cases that expert advice is necessary, but it is also in such cases that the delinquent behaviour is most difficult to correct. The final truth must be stated in this way, that the greater part of the educational burden must be carried by the remedial community itself, and that individual attention must be given only at those points where the child is obviously not participating easily, almost unconsciously, in the communal life.

I believe there is one more important thing that must be said about the modern reformatory method. It is still widely supposed that the prime function of the reformatory is to imprint on the tender mind the great lesson that crime does not pay. It is supposed that this can be done by strictness, hardness, austerity and deprivation. But it is quite wrong to suppose that a child is delinquent solely because he has lacked this kind of treatment. A child is more often delinquent because he has been deprived of other and far more fundamental needs, of security, affection, and outlets for his creative and emotional impulses. The change in him is remarkable when these deep needs are satisfied. His insolence, secretiveness, untimely independence, disobedience, disappear when he lives in the kind of community in which he finds, consciously or unconsciously, a meaning and purpose for his own life. It is quite wrong to suppose that the privileges and opportunities of an institution are evidences of pampering and sentimental benevolence. They are designed to restore self-reliance, self-respect and self-trust. They are tests of growth, providing a wealth of information in regard to the way in which the child is responding to remedial measures.

4. THE ROLE AND PURPOSE OF PUNISHMENT

It is time to bring the Diepkloof story to a close, but it would not be complete if it did not deal with two sub-themes. One is the role and purpose of punishment, both in an institution and in society itself. The other is to attempt to answer the questions, how far could Diepkloof Reformatory be said to have succeeded in its reformatory task? And how can one possibly judge the success of such an institution?

What is the place of punishment in the educational institution, and in society itself? Many people hold the view that punishment should be *retributive*. If an offender has inflicted hurt, then he should be hurt also. The extreme example of retributive punishment is the death penalty. Imprisonment can also be regarded as retributive. The official statements of judges and magistrates show clearly that many of them hold the belief that the punishment they inflict is retribution for the hurt or damage done by the offender. On the other hand, the idea of retributive punishment has to a large degree fallen into disfavour among educators. Some educators would regard retributive punishment as totally worthless. In many countries corporal punishment is forbidden. In some countries where it has been forbidden there has been a demand among teachers and prison officers that it should be restored, on the grounds that its abolition has created grave disciplinary problems. The attitudes of schoolboys towards corporal punishment are varied; some resent it bitterly, others take it as a joke.

A second view of punishment, not necessarily exclusive of the first, is that it is *deterrent*. Its purpose is not only to deter the offender, it is also to deter others who might be tempted to commit a similar offence. If the punishment succeeds in its purpose, then it is socially valuable. I was punished at the age of six for pushing a little girl off the pavement by being made to eat my lunch on the girls' verandah. I never did such a thing again, but I was deterred, not by the actual punishment, but by the attention which I had attracted to myself. That was the idea behind the use of the stocks in bygone times. Yet of course there are offenders who appear to be indifferent to public attention or public disapproval.

There is a third view of punishment, that it should be *reformatory*. This view has gained much ground in this century. If this view is held, then the word 'punishment' becomes inappropriate and is replaced by the word 'treatment'. The whole purpose of the transfer of the reformatories of South Africa from the Department of Prisons to the Department of Education was to change their goal from one of detention to one of education.

There is a fourth and last view of punishment, and that is that there need be none at all. Steps are taken against an offender for one reason and one reason only, and that is for the protection of society. If society does not need protection, then such persons need not be punished. They should merely be 'treated' in such a way as will remove their threat to society.

Diepkloof Reformatory inherited a system of punishment in which the infliction of cuts played the major role, largely because there were so few privileges that could be removed. These were – if I remember rightly – the withholding of a weekly spoonful of jam that was awarded after so many months, the withholding of sugar or some other item of diet, the withholding of the right to attend the Reformatory football matches. Another punishment, more drastic, was the ordering of solitary confinement, with or without spare diet, which was usually reserved for brutal and dangerous actions.

The decision to issue tobacco and to abolish the offence of smoking, except for boys under sixteen, and except for the leaves and seeds of the plant *cannabis* known to us as *dagga*, reduced the number of offences drastically, and reduced the number of cuts by about seventy per cent. We discussed at our staff meetings the pros and cons of corporal punishment, and it was clear that among both white and black staffs there was a strong feeling against abolition. It was finally decided to retain it for offences against the person and particularly when the person was a member of the staff, or when a boy absolutely refused to obey lawful orders. This was a rare offence indeed, and could be due to mental disturbance; therefore such punishment was never inflicted except on the advice of our visiting district surgeon.

Here I remember a story of another of our young white recruits from the Special Service Battalion. His name was Chris Botha, and he was another master of discipline. In his *span* was a boy Hendrik who refused to work. Sometimes he had to be carried in and out of the yard. Chris Botha advised against punishment, and gave it as his opinion that there was a deep-seated cause for this behaviour. Hendrik was sent to the hospital, and a week later he was dead. The postmortem revealed an internal growth the size of a small football.

Even today when I have reached the age of seventy-seven, I am unable to decide whether corporal punishment for a brutal offence achieves any good purpose. Such offences are often committed in what appear to be uncontrollable fits of rage, and it is highly improbable that the memory of corporal punishment will prevent another outburst. Sometimes the reformatory community would be outraged by a brutal offence committed on one of its number, as when for example a powerful older boy inflicted grievous injuries on a small one, and especially if the small one was a boy of nine or ten years of age. What kind of notice does authority take of such an offence? Does one do nothing, except reprimand perhaps? Solitary confinement seemed to be the only alternative to corporal punishment, but I developed a far greater aversion to confinement than to punishment.

And I held the belief that the infliction of corporal punishment made reparation for the outrage that the community had suffered. That the community could also take a sadistic delight in the punishment is also undoubted.

I still cannot make up my mind about the death penalty. South Africa executes more killers than any other country in what is called the 'free world'. The overwhelming majority of these are black. Some of these killers are robbers who will kill without mercy any person who resists them. Others are young black men who make their living on the congested black trains and buses that take black workers to and from the white cities. If we leave aside the question of personal responsibility, these killers are the product of a corrupting society, and it is this corrupting society that kills them in return.

George rose to be the senior house-captain of the main reformatory. He was a man, not a boy, powerful in build, and powerful in personality also. He made up his mind that while he was in the reformatory, and especially while he was the senior house-captain, he would obey authority, and what is more, that he would rule firmly and justly. Yet while he was in this position, he was already planning his first operation. This was to be the breaking into and robbing of the Comptonville Store, which was situated on the southern boundary of the Diepkloof Farm, and was guarded at night by a gentle black man called Theophilus. On the day after George's release, he and two companions broke into the Comptonville Store. Theophilus was not knocked unconscious; he was hacked to pieces, one of these pieces being his head. George and his two accomplices were sentenced to death and nothing in me rose to protest against it. On the day after the murder, and before it was known who had committed it, Engelbrecht brought for my signature the final report we had made on George, in which we predicted that he would soon again commit a merciless deed of this nature.

Was George responsible for his actions? If one takes the extreme behaviouristic view that we are all automatons, and that we respond to stimuli, that mind and conscience are man-made words that describe states or organs that do not exist, then George was not responsible. Was George *in part* responsible for his actions? That too is a question impossible to answer. In fact a belief in responsibility is very like a belief in God; one holds it because one chooses to hold it, it is in fact a *faith*, and is based on 'the evidence of things not seen'. As I have written earlier, I hold myself responsible for my actions, even while I accept that I am not in full control of them. But I choose not to believe that I have *no* control over them.

It seems to me impossible to find any moral justification for punishment unless one acknowledges the doctrine of personal responsibility. But there are occasions on which the court of law is willing to accept a doctrine of diminution of responsibility, and also occasions on which the court finds what are known as 'mitigating circumstances'. We are in a way dealing with a secret whose truth is hidden from us. Therefore, although I shudder at the thought of a corrupting society that punishes and even kills those whom it has corrupted, I have never been able to make up my mind finally about punishment, and especially the death penalty. If I were a ruler, I think I would incline strongly to the view that 'punishment' is to be used only for the protection of society.

5. HOW SUCCESSFUL WAS DIEPKLOOF?

Now for the question, how successful was Diepkloof as a reformatory? Does a reformatory ever reform anyone? I have no doubt that a good reformatory can stop a boy in a criminal career and send him off in another direction. It can take a small boy off the streets and away from the markets for three or four formative years, so that in a sense he becomes a different being. Diepkloof took Majohnnie off the streets of Kimberley for two or three years, and he became a model of industry and punctuality; he himself said that if he had gone back to Kimberley, he would have returned to the delinquent life. Yet I do not suppose that Diepkloof *remade* him; it merely encouraged the growth of hungers and aspirations that were there already.

In any case how does one measure success? It can only be done in an arbitrary manner. One can say that a boy has succeeded if he can last two years outside without committing a further offence, or without committing a further offence that could be called criminal; for in South Africa many black offences are purely statutory. If this arbitrary measurement was to be used, then Diepkloof was between fifty per cent and sixty per cent successful.

But even here the word 'successful' must be qualified. A reformatory catering for boys from nine to fifteen years of age will always be more successful than one for boys between sixteen and twenty-one. A reformatory for first offenders will always be more successful than one for second and third offenders. Some of Diepkloof's success must be attributed to the fact that the reformatory was used by magistrates and judges for boys who would have gone to orphanages, farm schools, industrial schools had such places been available. But in South Africa the number of alternative institutions for black boys is extremely small.

I shall close this Diepkloof story with an account of our staff discussions on the purpose, scope, usefulness of the punishment of offences. For many of our staff it was their first introduction to any kind of psychology or sociology or philosophy. Some of them were totally fascinated. Many of them had thought of punishment as the right and proper consequence of an offence. A person offended and he was punished. Whether the punishment had any detrimental or beneficial effect on the offender was almost irrelevant. But now these young white men were working at an institution for black boys and this institution was styled a 'reformatory'. It was therefore intended that the 'punishment' or the 'treatment' should be beneficial. This gave to them a new understanding of the work that had been thrust upon them as a result of the economic recession of the early 1930s. It was the kind of work that few of them would have chosen to do.

I regret only one thing, and that is that I was never able to listen in when they were trying to explain to sceptical parents, uncles and aunts, brothers and sisters, old school friends that they were in fact engaged on a task of national importance. The black supervisory staff had little difficulty in grasping that the reformatory had no punitive role to play. Its sole task was re-education. What made this new idea easier for them to accept was the fact that the work was being done for the children of their own people.

6. THE LAST WORD

I shall close this brief discussion of the personal and impersonal influences that operate within the institution, and this evaluation of direct and indirect methods of guidance and education, with a story which my colleague Dr van Antwerpen told against himself. He was a qualified minister of the Nederduitse Gereformeerde Kerk and he was appointed as Vice-Principal of the Coloured Reformatory of Tokai, just outside Cape Town. He expected much from the evangelistic sermon, and on his first Sunday he preached to his captive congregation, several hundreds strong. He thought his sermon was good and effective, and when it was finished he asked his hearers if they had any questions to ask. When they did not respond, he said to them encouragingly, 'You may ask anything you wish.' And a boy stood up at the back and said, *'Meneer, asseblief 'n stukkie twak.'*